Praise for **USERS**

"*Users* creeps upon the reader like the well-designed programs it describes, disguising itself as a tome about the future, virtual reality, the tech world, and what tantalizing dangers it wreaks. But what is truly frightening about this extraordinary book is the center of its futuristic shell—an unsettling look at marriage, parenting, and relationships that will lurk in the reader's mind long after the final page. Colin Winnette has written a delicious nightmare. Welcome to its open maw."

—Esmé Weijun Wang, author of
The Collected Schizophrenias

"The best kind of book: both thrillingly old-fashioned and utterly, daringly timely. Winnette captures the anxiety and paranoia of the current age in a tale that will have you ripping through the pages. Haunting, clever, witty, terrifying, moving; reader, I loved it."

—Andrew Sean Greer, author of *Less*,
winner of the 2018 Pulitzer Prize for Fiction

"A surreal puzzle box and page-turner from which the reader may never recover, full of the unique absurdity, dark humor, and character insight that make Colin Winnette's work such a joy."

—Jeff Vandermeer, *New York Times*
bestselling author of the Southern Reach trilogy
and *Hummingbird Salamander*

"In gripping prose and disturbingly sharp focus, Colin Winnette presents us with a not-too-distant future where technology and selfhood have become completely entangled. *Users* shows how we can become addicted to our customizable versions of reality, both on- and offline—and how tenuous the boundary between these two realms can be. I kept thinking about this novel long after I put it down."

—Hernan Diaz, Pulitzer Prize finalist, author of *In the Distance* and *Trust*

"An engaging story of a virtual reality designer stuck in a rut . . . In Winnette's hands, the dangerous blur between the virtual and reality provides both a warning and a thrill." —*Publishers Weekly*

Praise for **THE JOB OF THE WASP**

"*The Job of the Wasp* is wonderfully creepy and peculiar . . . Colin Winnette is an enviable, natural talent, and to read him is a pure entertainment."

—Patrick deWitt, author of *French Exit* and *The Sisters Brothers*

"A witty and grisly gothic unlike anything I've ever read. You should absolutely read this." —Kelly Link, author of *Get in Trouble*

users

users

a novel

colin winnette

soft skull
new york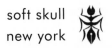

First Soft Skull edition: 2023

Library of Congress Cataloging-in-Publication Data
Names: Winnette, Colin, author.
Title: Users : a novel / Colin Winnette.
Description: First Soft Skull edition. | New York : Soft Skull Press, 2023.
Identifiers: LCCN 2022038557 | ISBN 9781593767372 (hardcover) | ISBN 9781593767389 (ebook)
Classification: LCC PS3623.I66345 U74 2023 | DDC 813/.6—dc23
LC record available at https://lccn.loc.gov/2022038557

Jacket design by Gregg Kulick
Jacket illustration © iStock / Lera Danilova
Book design by Wah-Ming Chang

Published by Soft Skull Press
New York, NY
www.softskull.com

Printed in the United States of America

10 9 8 7 6 5 4 3 2 1

For Andi

part one

the beginning

YOUR HEART WILL STOP

Miles was getting death threats. So far, fewer than he would have liked. Not that he wanted to be getting death threats, but once he started seeing them for what they were, he felt like having a few more, from a few more people, would somehow be less threatening.

Technically, this first one wasn't the first. It was the first he'd noticed. The first he'd recognized as a legitimate death threat.

SOON

That was all the real first threat had said. He was sure he wasn't alone in his capacity to misinterpret the message. It was only a word, and words came alive in context. They relied on one another; the difference between a log and a log cabin.

YOUR HEART WILL STOP

The messages were letter-pressed on weighted stationery—not tossed off online in a fit of pique. There was no postmark on either envelope, no return address. Someone had spent time, actual money. They had carried the notes to his home, slid them in the mail slot, and left.

✦

When Miles's daughters arrived home from school to find him staring at the refrigerator, they absently asked about the new artwork mounted to its door.

"It's a reminder," he told them. "A note to myself."

"It's pretty," said his six-year-old, fingering the edge of the cream-colored paper.

Miles had placed a kitchen magnet on the bottom half of the threat, so the top half became a flap that could conceal or reveal the message with a touch. He guided his daughter's hand from the flap before she could lift it.

But she was right. It was pretty. The quality of the stationery was part of the reason he'd overlooked the first threat.

SOON

Seeing the envelope, he'd mistaken it for a wedding invitation. Opening it, he'd amended the mistake, guessing it was advance notice for a forthcoming save-the-date.

YOUR HEART WILL STOP

There was no longer room for misinterpretation. *Soon*
finally had a context. *Soon* was when his heart would stop.

Miles's wife came home late, as she'd been doing more and more often. She found Miles in the kitchen, still staring at the folded note on the refrigerator door.

"I'm tired," she said, hanging her purse from a chair back and immediately beginning to undress.

"What would you do if someone killed me?" he said.

"If who killed you?" she said.

"Anyone," he said.

"Honestly," she said, "it would depend on the person. How and why they did it."

"That's it?" he said.

"That's all you've given me," she said, vanishing down the dark hall.

Miles stared at the threat for a moment, before calling after her. "You're saying there's a version where you'd have no reaction at all?"

"That's not what I'm saying," she called back. "I'm saying the reaction would be different, depending on those things."

Miles got up and followed his wife into the bedroom, where he could hear her fiddling with a drawer.

"What's an example of a possible reaction, then?" he said. "Hypothetically."

"I already told you," she said. She slid the drawer shut. "I'd need all the variables."

✦

Before tonight, Miles had made a project of letting go. He'd been trying to live more in the moment, to accept things as they came. While he rejected mindfulness as a practice, he still allowed himself to deploy certain mindful strategies when convenient. But now Miles was mindful only of the threat.

He spent most of the night in the kitchen with it, realizing again and again that it was still there. Still real. Still a death threat.

SOON

A moment of self-doubt sent him digging through the trash for the first note. He was no longer sure he remembered it correctly. Was that really all it said? He knew the search was futile—how many times had they taken out the trash in the last few days—but he couldn't not check after having had the thought. If the note was still there, he wanted to know. He wanted to be certain. He wanted to consider both notes at the same time, see them for exactly what they were, and understand exactly how they were working together to make him feel the way he was feeling. Miles felt afraid. He felt uncertain. He felt like there was something he should be doing to stop all this, but he had not figured it out yet.

Miles's hand came out of the trash can's liner with nothing but a yellow grain of rice stuck under his nail. His best guess was the Mediterranean they'd ordered weeks ago. They'd taken out the trash countless times since then, and goddamn grains of rice were still showing up. He rinsed his hands and gave up on the trash. Miles was irritable. It was almost two in the morning.

✦

When Miles found he couldn't sleep, he searched online for a database of toll-free hotlines offering sympathetic ears to those experiencing harassment or abuse. He wasn't comfortable labeling the two letters he'd received on expensive stationery "harassment" or "abuse," but it felt astute to recognize these letters might prefigure harassment or abuse of some kind, and he wanted to be ready.

Minutes later, a young operator was telling him that fear and frustration were completely valid and natural feelings.

"It might comfort you to know," she said, "that the statistical likelihood of anyone following through on a written threat is low. Even so, I understand why you can't help but take them seriously. Unfortunately, legal recourse is limited in situations like these. At least at this stage. Even if the author of the notes were to show up, the options available to you would depend on how that person acted. What they said and did. The truth is, you'll have to wait and see. Though I imagine that's less comforting than you'd like it to be."

She sounded young to Miles—far too young for her to be so well versed in death-threat best practices. But something in her short life so far had led her to become an expert at navigating situations Miles had only just been introduced to—not conceptually, but personally—and that even he could acknowledge he wasn't handling particularly well. It didn't seem fair.

"You're sure you don't know who could be sending them?" she said.

"Like who?" he said. "I don't know anyone like that."

"Of course," she said. She waited a moment before continuing. "The source may become clear with time, or it may not. But I can tell you from experience that in the meantime you'll swing between worry, forgetting, frustration, anger. Depression. It's normal. It's valid. If it's any consolation, in the grand scheme of things, what you're dealing with is relatively minor."

It wasn't much of a consolation—if anything, Miles felt demoted—but at least according to a professional his situation wasn't urgent. If it wasn't an emergency, that meant his inaction so far may well have been the best possible response. Somehow, instinctively, he'd gotten it right.

"You're right," he said. "You must hear so much worse."

The operator laughed, then caught herself and folded the sound into an abrupt clearing of her throat. But it was too late. In that brief and vulnerable moment Miles caught a glimpse of unknown depths, and he was suddenly gripped by the need to hear every detail she had to offer from her years of experience on the job, every story from every call that would put his situation in perspective, tip the scales, and sort the unwieldy card he'd been dealt back into the deck of relative normalcy.

"Unfortunately," she said, having replaced all discernible candor with an affected neutrality, likely the product of some weekend orientation, "unfortunately, these situations do escalate. Not always, and typically when they do there are precipitating incidents. A breakup. A fight. A restraining order. But in the absence of those things, anonymous letters are rarely acted on. They often cease as abruptly as they start. For your purposes, it's best to assume they mean nothing until you have reason to think otherwise."

Miles tried to imagine what those reasons to think otherwise might be, but the second the images began to populate his mind, he banished them.

"So it could get worse," he said, "but there's nothing I can do about it. Nothing I *should* do. No way to prepare. That's what you're saying? I just want to be clear: I do nothing about the death threats."

"For now," she said, "the best thing is to focus on your daily life. Try not to let the anxiety this is causing you take over. Do you meditate? If not, try it. Try focusing on what's in front of you as you move through the day, one thing at a time. With any luck, this will all be over soon." It was a sober script prepared off-mic, written specifically to handle people like Miles, people who were not used to the idea of looming violence, of inevitable violence, of other humans in the world who would like to harm, specifically, them.

"If you're worried, and you can afford it," she said, without the slightest hint of discovery in her voice, "you might invest in a security system. Lock your doors. Stay vigilant. But in all likelihood, nothing will come of the notes."

More than frightening, it was unsatisfying—the notion that the best course of action was to continue resisting action at all. While he was happy to have been right in his instincts so far, it didn't seem like a viable long-term strategy to continue doing nothing. Miles liked to think of himself as capable of this kind of rational and detached problem-solving . . . but these were death threats! Maybe things wouldn't progress, but if they did it was hard to imagine them progressing in any way other than the stated design, an undesirable outcome, in the face of which Miles would feel foolish to have done nothing preventive.

"I'm sorry to interrupt," he said as she began her sign-off spiel. *Remember, we're always here.* "I don't mean to keep you. I'm just having trouble wrapping my head around the idea of how exactly one does nothing. If I sit and wait, as you're suggesting, aren't I simply handing the situation over to my would-be assailant, rather than actively working to determine my fate?"

The operator was slow to answer, flipping pages in some laminated manual, no doubt, or mentally preparing herself to spend another hour looping back through responses to the same concerns Miles had been approaching from different angles for the past hour. Hearing her hesitation, he felt guilty for leaning on her. This young woman wasn't even getting paid to answer calls like his, to talk strangers like him through their preliminary responses to anonymous threats, general harassment, persistent stalkers, life-shattering assaults. Whatever *worse* meant. She must have lived through something unimaginable to want to spend her nights telling people it was normal, understandable even, to be afraid all the time. According to her, it was supposed to be a comforting thought: the standard validity of his fear. Maybe the more you said these things, the easier they were to accept as true. Or maybe they simply were true, and some people had no choice but to know that and work from there.

"You're not keeping me," she said. "And no, I'm not talking about doing nothing. I'm talking about doing the work of trying to find your way back to the parts of your life that make you happy, acknowledging and accepting the fact that there are other parts you can't control."

"And I'll feel better," said Miles, "once I've done that?"

"Some days will be harder than others," she said. "Some days will be easier. In either case, we're always here."

He understood they'd yet again reached the end of the loop, but he didn't feel finished. He wasn't ready to be alone. Still, his options were few: start it all over again or let her go.

"Okay," he said.

"It's frustrating," she said, "I know. That's a completely natural and valid way to feel. It might comfort you to know that the statistical likelihood of anyone following through on a written threat is very low. In all likelihood, none of this will feel all that important to you in a matter of time. You'll have other things to worry about, to focus on. If that turns out to not be the case, we're always here."

✦

Miles washed his hands, took out the garbage, and washed his hands again. In bed, he could smell the cubes of lamb that had nested on the rice maybe two weeks prior. He kept his hands at his sides, pushing them deep under the covers, as far from his nose as he could get them. The smell remained. It seemed to fill the room.

All that, thought Miles, from a single grain of rice.

The note was still on the fridge in the morning. Some part of Miles had hoped it wouldn't be. Not that it would have vanished in the night—that was too creepy—but that it would never have been there in the first place. That it was a dream, or a vision delivered upon him in the throes of a fit of insomnia.

Everyone else was energized by a good night's sleep. His six-year-old was drawing lines through the salt she'd spilled on the table, and his ten-year-old was at the stove, announcing she'd be making breakfast for the family.

"Pancakes," she said, fiddling with the knob for the burner. She was occupying herself by turning it past the quick flick of the igniter, pumping a spurt of gas into the room, then quickly turning it back to OFF.

"There's no time for cleanup," said his wife. "Honey, move."

He was at the fridge door, blocking it. He'd meant to open it—for what, he couldn't remember now—but he'd become sidetracked by the note yet again. For several minutes, he'd been standing there, lifting the flap to read the message, then letting the top half fall back into place.

"Sorry," he said. He stepped aside so his wife could get water from the filter.

"What is that?" she said, pointing at the paper.

"A death threat," he said.

"Funny," she said. She slid a carton of fat brown eggs from the bottom shelf and turned. "How many eggs can you fry in ten minutes?"

Across the room, his ten-year-old was grinning like a maniac.

"I could fry them all," she said.

At work, Miles had a different problem. Their user community was in revolt.

"It's the fucking *Ghost Lover*," said Lily, the only person in the office speaking above a whisper.

His other coworkers were at their desks working quietly—an alarming start to any day. Miles knew from years of working at the company that the calmer the place seemed when he arrived, the worse, and farther reaching, the underlying issue.

"The nerds are up in arms about it," Lily said. She followed Miles into the office kitchen as he sped through his morning routine, preparing himself for the shitstorm headed his way. "They're claiming it breaks our code of conduct."

Thursdays were normally "no meeting" days, and Miles had gone in planning to catch up on all the small projects he'd previously set aside in favor of short conversations that would inevitably run long about larger projects he ultimately had nothing to do with. One quick glance at his calendar, however, revealed it was already clogged with meeting requests, starting thirty minutes before he'd arrived and running through the end of the day.

"We don't have a code of conduct," said Miles, pumping half a cup of pure cream into his coffee from a refrigerated bag. "Right?"

"Not for *our* stuff," she said. "But we've been deleting user experiences."

He raised an eyebrow.

"Oh, fuck off," said Lily. "I'm talking about racist shit. Sexist shit. Users are building fucking rape dungeons, Miles. We shouldn't need a code of conduct to justify banning that shit."

"I didn't say anything," he said, heading back to his desk.

"That was a shitload of cream," said Lily, keeping pace.

✦

Lily was right about the cream. It *was* a shitload. But lately, a shitload was the bare minimum required to get Miles through each morning and into the first part of his day. His shirts were getting tighter. When he turned and pinched himself in front of the mirror, there was a line of fat developing at the base of his back like the inflatable bumpers at a bowling alley. He knew it was an indulgence—and one in which he partook too often to justify as self-care—but his resolve to curb the impulse routinely collapsed under the recognition that the cream was the only reliable source of pleasure available to him on any given day. He looked forward to it. He missed it when he didn't have it. Some days he would drink small amounts straight from a cup, provided no one was there to witness him doing it. Either way, the coffee had become secondary.

The company had the cream driven in each week from a farm two hours north of the city. Miles had fallen in love with it the day they'd visited the farm on a work field trip. An "off-site," they'd called it, which made it sound more professional, more productive, than the company had any intention of it being. On the drive up, his manager had passed out tiny personal bottles of champagne, because, in truth, the off-site was designed to be little more than a display of the luxuries the company could afford to offer its employees, while still turning a healthy profit. It was marketing, meant just as much for those who would hopefully hear about it as those who had been forced to attend. The whole thing was absurd without being funny. It was programmatically unhinged, and it had all the subtlety of a third date.

Miles had been silently, invisibly, averse to the outing from the moment they were loaded onto the black buses, logging all his complaints in the back of his mind for later that night, when he would unload them on his wife, rapid-fire, over wine. But all that changed when a ranch hand in pressed Dickies served Miles a dollop of pure cream from a Dixie cup the size of an acorn. The moment he tasted it, his aversion to the trip melted away. The cream was vaguely vegetal, with the fatty lightness of good cake. To Miles, it tasted like fresh air, a life without cars. It was the mucus of the gods, and it transformed the burdensome trip into a divine gift in his eyes. Miles sipped the small serving and asked for another, confident the day had reached its peak. Then he was introduced to the source.

Moments later, a knot of healthy cows chewing clockwise approached a fence where Miles stood. He reached out, touched one on its wet pink nose. Their names were written in chalk on a tablet hung from a nearby post. Miles called out the name he liked most, Lefty, and a brown cow with a chipped ear lifted its massive anvil of a head to look back at him.

"Miles," said Lily, snapping in his face. "Where the fuck are you?"

Miles had been staring open-mouthed into the middle of the room, fiddling with the bottom jaw of a Godzilla head someone had left on his desk overnight. He checked its mouth for a death threat, then wondered if the head itself was the threat.

"Sorry," he said. He shoved his hands into his pockets and tried to remember what they were talking about. "We didn't see any of this coming?" he said.

"I think we underestimated how mad they'd be when we shut down the fucking rape dungeons," she said. "And how organized."

Right.

"Dream it and it's yours," he said.

"Dream it and it's yours," she said.

19

✦

They'd group-tested the slogan for weeks, but everyone had known it was the one the moment it slid out of an intern's mouth. *Dream it and it's yours.* What better way to position a virtual reality company that put you, the user, in the creative driver's seat?

More than simple interactivity, users had control over their environment entirely, from start to finish. Every reproducible element, at least. It was a living fantasy, limited only by the speed of your internet and the company's servers.

The only trouble, or the first sign of trouble when they were just getting started, was that users seemed to have impoverished dreams. Rather than flying over the Grand Canyon dropping water balloons on ex-presidents, they were building experiences for themselves that consisted primarily of things they could already do in the real world: sitting in a bathtub at home, petting their cat, eating dinner with a faceless pack of abs, or, a real stretch, shopping with a celebrity. The problem was that users were boring more than the company with these outings—they were boring themselves. They weren't coming back to the platform, and when they did, they were staying for less and less time. And the less time users spent on the platform, the less valuable the platform was to shareholders, advertisers, and potential investors. To survive, the company needed users to stay put, to keep dreaming, but as it turned out, the unlimited possibilities of their dreams weren't enough to keep the average person's attention for very long.

The early days of the platform had shown the company how hard it was for most users to dive headfirst into their own imaginations—to independently sustain an engaging and prolonged projection for long enough to keep the company afloat. To do that, the users needed a boost, a little nudge toward the deep end. They needed a place to start.

The company hit paydirt when they began releasing their own content, designed in-house. *Alternative realities* sounded too dystopian, because each was only meant to be a jumping-off point, not the destination. They were more like the ON button for a dream—or a drug that invites the hallucination, then hands over the reins. After months of user testing, the company landed on the name Original Experiences.

The Ghost Lover was the company's most popular Original Experience by far. In it, you were you, in your apartment or home, with things almost exactly as they were in your daily life, only you were being haunted by the ghost of an ex-lover. The experience was designed to create the feeling that the haunting was deeply personal. That your specific Ghost Lover was entirely your own, built from your life experiences, tailored to your tastes and behavior. There was a massive onboarding process to help achieve this effect, but the onboarding process itself was part of the deception. The company had learned that asking a series of penetrating personal questions before a user began would grant a generic ghost the air of specificity. The more broadly the ghost behaved, the more room was left for users to project onto it, and the more time a user sank into answering questions about their ghost, the more generous their interpretations of its broad behavior would be. It was an easy trick, and one the company had learned early on, thanks again to user testing. The *less* specific the company was in its design, the more specifically tailored users seemed to think the experience was. Again, it wasn't that users didn't have imaginations. Their imaginations needed help.

There was a flood of creativity after the first wave of OEs hit. Daily users almost doubled, and the community library shelves were soon bloated with strange new user-generated experiences. There was something almost confessional about them. Memories were a common model—monumental moments in a user's life. The dreams spun out from there. Increasingly, the new experiences took on the qualities of fantasy, merging elements of real life with the impossible logic of the subconscious. These were the road maps the company had been hoping to access all along. The extra-rational. The indescribably personal. Some key that could help unlock the cognitive processes behind the construction of a fantasy. The cultivation of unchecked want. Pure desire. As it turned out, the key had been little more than suggestion.

To act as free as they truly were, users needed something to riff on, an example of what was possible. They needed to know what it could look like, and they needed something external, something beyond themselves, to confirm that the choices they'd made were of consequence. Once they were hooked, each user became a derrick, spewing the oil of good, reliable, marketable data.

✦

"What's a rape dungeon got to do with *The Ghost Lover?*" said Miles.

"It's a consent issue," said Lily.

"What's that mean?" said Miles.

"You might want to workshop that before the hearings," said Lily.

Miles tried to remember what happened in *The Ghost Lover.* There were some opportunities for dancing in the later chapters, but they'd never gone full porno with it. In fact, that was what set them apart from almost every other leading virtual reality company out there, though the absence of explicit sexual content was far from a puritanical effort on the company's part. As they saw it, the proposition of sex overpowered the operating systems behind an individual's natural dream construction.

"A bush in the hand beats imagining birds," was how one of the finance guys explained it at parties.

Despite its title, *The Ghost Lover* had never been about sex. Originally, Miles had wanted to make a melancholic experience. Something internal. A curiously infinite navel. He'd pulled the idea together over a long weekend, while his wife and kids were in the desert taking photos of nightmare bugs and glittering rock formations. Miles had been waking up each night to the sound of thumps in his wall, like someone nearby was struggling to move furniture. The sound was always the same. Too regular to be incidental, but too inconsistent to be something like a washing machine. Maybe it was the fact that he hadn't been alone for more than a night since his second daughter was born, but he hadn't been able to shake the feeling that the source of the thumps was supernatural, like something from beyond was trying to use the wall to communicate with him. It was a ridiculous idea, but it had lodged itself in his mind. Alone with his fears, and in the absence of other, more reasonable explanations, Miles had spent hours online reading ghost stories to better understand why a ghost might be hiding in his walls. He'd found hundreds of threads on the subject, supposedly firsthand accounts by people who had encountered ghosts in their homes—specifically, ghosts in their walls. Most of the time, these ghosts didn't cause any trouble. They weren't aggrieved souls come to set things right. They were confused, or lost, or lonely, read the reports, stuck inside the walls like a cat.

Miles lay awake in bed later that night, listening to the thumps in his wall, more intently now that it was something he'd spent time reading about. Rather than clarifying the situation or putting him at ease, however, his experience online had only complicated his uneasiness, and in the absence of a readily available answer or plan of action, he wanted nothing but to be rid of his concerns altogether. He didn't believe in ghosts, and he knew he didn't care enough about the question to devote any more of his time to it—but the possibility, the not knowing, was eating away at him. All he wanted at this point was to sleep.

The later it got, the clearer it became to Miles that, in order to let this all go, to be free of the burden of his ignorance regarding the potential reality of ghosts, he would need to either answer the question definitively, to once and for all find a satisfactory explanation for a question no one in the history of humankind had managed to satisfactorily explain, or turn his experience of the thumps—and the subsequent questions and fears their inexplicable existence inspired in him—into something that could be passed on to someone else. That way, the whole thing could be forgotten, or at least its potency could be reduced.

As his mother used to put it, "A burden shared is a burden halved."

Miles didn't remember sleeping, but he woke the next morning to find a wet dream had given him the final piece of the puzzle, like a cold and glutinous splash of lightning. The thumps, plus the subconscious emission, equaled *The Ghost Lover*. An experience just south of actual life, but with real-world implications. He hoped it would reconnect users to their pasts, open them up to the world of ghosts as he understood it, or as the internet had tried to explain it to him. Then, wherever he was, he would no longer be alone there, and he would finally be able to get some sleep.

Miles had been on the hook for an Original Experience for several months at this point, so once the idea occurred to him, he ran with it. He designed and launched *The Ghost Lover* in a month, sleeping undisturbed every night since he'd arrived at the concept. Following its quiet release, the experience unexpectedly took off, replacing their second-most-popular OE within a few days and remaining on top for just over a year, before finally losing out to *The Royal Punishment*. For sheer retention, *The Ghost Lover* hovered comfortably between second and third highest since its release, depending on what was newly published to the platform week to week.

Miles couldn't fathom how something that trivial, that personal and incidental, had years later managed to become the center of a company-wide controversy, but if there was some fatal flaw he hadn't thought through well enough at the outset, it was because he had been encouraged to produce the experience as quickly as possible. And when it turned out to be surprisingly successful, there was of course no call to go back and think it through retroactively. At least there hadn't been before now.

"There's no . . ." Miles paused. He cupped his palms, then brought them as close together as possible without letting them touch, not knowing what exactly it was meant to signify, but hoping it got the point across to Lily while remaining SFW.

Lily only smirked, so he brought his hands behind his back.

"Physical intimacy," he continued, "in *The Ghost Lover.*

It wasn't designed that way. If someone changed something, or added something problematic, we should revert it. It was fine before. I don't understand why people can't leave well enough alone."

"Calm down," said Lily. "No one fucked with your ghost. The argument is that *haunting*, at least as it occurs in *The Ghost Lover*, is nonconsensual."

"For who?" he said. "You or the ghost?"

"Take your pick," she said. "There are camps arguing either side. By not making itself explicitly known, by not making contact in a straightforward way, the ghost allows no opportunities for the main character, for you, to give direct, enthusiastic consent for any level of intimacy, which is a sticking point with some users. For others, the ghost comes off like a prisoner. After all, the ghost doesn't make a choice to haunt, or if it does, we don't see it. In the experience, haunting is simply the circumstance of the ghost's existence. The ghost has no other options. Therefore, any relationship it enters into with the main character, with you, is done under duress."

"Fine," he said. "If people don't like it, pull it. There are plenty of other OEs at this point." Miles knew it couldn't be that simple, but he wanted to know why without asking.

"You're a real fucking idiot," said Lily. She watched him like she was waiting for him to confirm that he understood what she meant. "I'm serious," she said. "All the way. Fucking. Stupid."

"All right," he said.

"People love it," she said. "I don't know why, but

people love the shit out of your dumb fucking ghost. It's our most popular experience by a yard, and widely replicated in user-generated material. Fucking morbid, if you ask me, but since you didn't, I'll tell you: the problem is, the fucking nerds feel that the experiences they're creating are being deleted for lesser or similar offenses, while yours remains one of the most popular experiences on the platform. They think it's unfair. At best, it's censorship. At worst, it's a scam. We create the illusion of a platform built around the contributions of users but delete any user-generated competition that threatens the popularity of our Original Experiences, that kind of thing. It couldn't be further from the truth, but we can't exactly defend ourselves by reminding the users that we own their so-called competition, and if anything they made ever came close to threatening the popularity of our OEs, we'd exercise that ownership by paying them pennies on the dollar to edit and repackage their stuff as our own. It doesn't exactly roll off the tongue. And if we just alter or delete *The Ghost Lover*, it hardly addresses the issue. They'll see right through it. What's worse, they'll start to think they have power over us. That we'll bend to their will whenever they get their fucking hackles up. So— Stop it."

She snapped twice in his face again, and Miles stopped fiddling with the Godzilla jaw.

"It's annoying as shit," she said.

"People are comparing the hauntings to rape dungeons?" he said.

Lily leaned on his desk with her left elbow and

exaggerated a yawn. Unlike everyone else on the floor, she didn't seem nervous about any of this. She seemed bored.

"Yeah," she said.

"You think it holds water?" he said.

"It doesn't fucking matter what we think," she said. "We lost twenty-five thousand users this morning. The hashtag KillTheDream was trending over the weekend."

"Shit," he said.

"*Shit's* fucking right," she said.

Miles raised the edge of his adjustable desk to meet his belly button, guiding Lily back into a standing position beside him. If it was going to be a long day, he could at least burn a few calories while he developed carpal tunnel. He opened his calendar and watched the rest of the meeting requests pour in.

"I'll let you get," said Lily, "to the shit."

"Hey," he said. She was halfway across the room already, and he had to raise his voice for her to hear him. "Have you been sending me notes?"

"The fuck for?" she said, loud enough to settle things.

5

WORKING LATE WON'T SAVE YOU

Back at home, Miles found the new note hidden between two pieces of junk mail: a credit card offer and a solicitation for higher monthly donations to a Southern civil rights advocacy group Miles had been supporting for years. According to his internal survival hierarchy, the death threat should have come first focus-wise, but Miles reminded himself of his vow to heed the advice of the harassment hotline's operator. *Focus on your daily life. Try not to let the anxiety this is causing you be all that you feel.* He turned his attention to the solicitation, the associated stresses of which he felt he could credibly argue were a part of his daily life.

Over the last six months, this particular civil rights advocacy group had been plagued with scandal. The trouble started with the leak of several private messages the head of the group had sent to underage women on social media. Miles had read them all and found them embarrassingly juvenile. *You are so hawt.* Not especially lewd, but too close to something Miles might have written as a teenager.

Miles had thought of this man as a better-educated representative of his own ideals. Someone who understood society's ills, now and historically. Not only that, but Miles had thought of this man as someone who knew the steps that needed to be taken toward a brighter future, as well as the most effective ways of mitigating the harm that could be done by evil men in the meantime. Confronted with new evidence as to what this supposedly great man got up to in his private life, Miles was now grappling with doubts as to whether or not any of what he'd once believed about this man had ever been true. Even if it was, the issue remained that Miles wasn't sure he could really take the guy seriously anymore.

Miles had kept his family's standing donation long after the civil rights leader had sloppily denounced the initial allegations then almost immediately released a ponderous apology after several of the messages were made public. The donations didn't feel good anymore, but there was a complicating wrinkle in the case that kept Miles from fully turning on the man—and therefore the group he still fronted—despite all the noise being made online. The wrinkle was: whatever the man had done, Miles wasn't sure he trusted the sincerity of the concern behind the initial leaks. It was hard to ignore the fact that these early reports had all come from conservative media outlets. Even if it didn't change his personal feelings about what the man had done, or his belief that the man had done these things, Miles suspected an underlying manipulation, and he was hesitant to allow himself to become part of the larger scheme. Though Miles believed the consequent outrage was fair—the man's behavior was illegal in some states, and at the very least an abuse of power— the sudden release of the messages, many of which dated back five or six years, smacked of other historical attempts to discredit and disgrace civil rights leaders growing in power. This man wasn't exactly a hero, but he had been doing good, quiet work. It just wasn't the only thing he'd been quietly doing.

After a week of corrosive disappointment, Miles caught himself wondering if the two things weren't mutually exclusive: if you couldn't be a dirtbag and a good lawyer. But the intellectual exercise didn't bring him anywhere he wanted to be. The moment Miles found himself sympathizing with this man, his chest would seize. His breath would lock in his lungs. While Miles understood that the condemnation of a man he'd never met had nothing to do with him personally, he still feared that the international response to this man's behavior was a good indicator of how people might come to think of him, of Miles, should they one day be bothered to unearth the thoughts he'd had, the urges he'd dispelled throughout his life, and, God willing, would continue to dispel. It pained him now— after he'd sat down and read them all—to think of these messages gridded across the front page of national newspapers, only then to be kicked around the internet forever.

If Miles had learned anything from working at a virtual reality company that invited users to build customized experiences out of the content of their dreams, it was that we all kept horrible parts of ourselves alive in the dark. The idea of having his own thoughts logged somewhere, only to be plucked out at some point in the future, scrutinized and examined anew, was enough to make him object to the idea behind the scandal, though not to the scandal itself. Miles knew a fundamental difference between him and this man was that, unlike Miles, this man hadn't just had the thoughts, he'd acted on them. This man had sent the messages, gotten other people involved—much younger people. The man wasn't being persecuted for his intentions; he was being prosecuted for acting on them, and for making them known. It was hard for Miles to argue with the idea of this man having to face consequences for his actions. But this mining of past selves still left him with nightmares of brain surgeons one day isolating his own felonious thoughts in the folds of his decomposing tissue, the wrinkles in his brain serving as archive to equivalently candid urges that more or less amounted to typo-riddled come-ons privately secreted to barely legal teens.

Miles honestly didn't know if he was a worse man in his mind than he was in his life. Or if the shame that flooded him at the sight of this other man's name was the consequence of a loose association he still felt with someone he'd once considered a representative of his own conscience. Miles objected to the idea that a reevaluation of this man, of his man—and by extension someday possibly himself—necessitated a reevaluation of the good that man had managed to accomplish at the same time as whatever else he was doing. If this man was now a pariah, what did that say about the enduring quality of good deeds? And what did it say about Miles? Who was worse, a bad man who'd done a few good things in his life, or a reportedly good man who, so far, had accomplished nothing?

It didn't help that, despite the uproar, the man was still a public figure. Still living a comfortable life. The world seemed to be saying one thing, doing another. Or there was a massive gap between the ideas being circulated in public and those persisting in private. Surely there was more to be done, but Miles didn't know what it was. In the past, he'd relied on men like this one to set the example. Now he was on his own.

Miles crumpled up the solicitation and squeezed it into the overfull recycling can. He could hear his daughters in the other room, playing a game and trying to keep their voices down now that he was home. It was nice to know he didn't have to keep a constant, watchful eye over them anymore. It had been a welcome surprise when his ten-year-old accepted the responsibility of watching her sister on nights like these—when he and his wife were both working late—without complaining or manifesting a level of excitement that would have alarmed him.

"Sure," she'd said.

Miles and his wife had argued for hours before asking her, with his wife making the case that her own sister had watched her at ten, while Miles had limply argued that these were different times, and ten was younger now than it had been then. At hour two of their argument, he'd come close to admitting that his objections had nothing to do with the times, or what ten was like for either generation of ten-year-olds, but had entirely to do with the fact that their ten-year-old sometimes scared him. He'd stopped himself, knowing his wife would demand evidence and he'd have none to give. His fear of his daughter was in response not to something she had done, but to what she might do. Plainly put, she had a weirdness about her that bordered on hostility. He didn't know where it came from, and he didn't know what to do about it. But it left him with the uneasy feeling that he didn't know exactly what she was capable of. His wife would undoubtedly argue that this sounded more like a *him* problem than a *her* problem. So Miles had gone on whimpering *different times*, and his wife had destroyed him, insisting ten was only different now if they allowed it to be different. If they constantly relieved their daughter of the responsibilities they didn't think she could handle, she would in fact never learn to handle those responsibilities.

Months later, it seemed his wife had been right. The girls were fine on their own, and Miles was relieved of the need to rush in and declare himself home or dismiss an overpriced babysitter at the end of every long night.

WORKING LATE WON'T SAVE YOU

The note was no doubt part of the death-threat series, but Miles found it oddly encouraging. He'd worked four hours past quitting time that night, retroactively piecing together ideas for a new code of conduct that would permit *The Ghost Lover* to remain on the company's platform as it was, while also clearly justifying the excision of the rape dungeons and other experiences of their ilk. He'd felt he was doing good work, making headway on the road to salvation—until he'd logged on and read the comments from the user community.

He'd wanted to better understand their complaints. The trouble was, they were extremely convincing. One user in particular, who seemed to be a pillar of the resistance—the one around whom tens of thousands of users rallied—made the elegant case that they had studied the issue closely and found no clear guidelines behind the deletions, or none that had been equally applied to the company's own Original Experiences. For this user, the problem had started with *The Ghost Lover* and its creator—with Miles—but only really made sense when you looked beyond *The Ghost Lover*. How different, this user argued, was *The Royal Punishment* from some of the lighter S&M dungeons that had been pulled down? While some of the user experiences deleted by the company had been offensive and dangerous, many were obvious expansions on scenarios written by the company itself. Yet the company and its creators were never held accountable. And, once you started tracking the deletions as a group, there were patterns to the deletions that exhibited a clear discomfort with specific religious groups, spiritual beliefs, and sexual preferences. Satanists were disproportionately punished over Christians. Hindus over Muslims. Open-world experiences centering polyamorous love seemed to be under scrutiny, while several polygamous experiences were skating by unmolested. Granted, there were fewer of these, but the general pattern of the data, even in the smallest corners of the platform, was hard to overlook. Finally, this user noted, though the company's language was queer-friendly and "inclusive," the deletions exhibited an obvious heteronormative bias. The user had therefore concluded that, while there was no doubt a guiding hand behind the decision-making process that led to these deletions, it certainly wasn't a user-friendly code of conduct. When you compared the targeted groups to user profiles, the biases expressed in the deletions simply didn't reflect the makeup of the user community at large. These deletions were being determined by something else, and this was what they, the users, were working to identify next—with or without the company's help.

Miles was impressed. The user had done their research.

Though it was never explicitly stated by anyone at the company, and they'd done their best to mask any behavior that directly reflected this reality, the company's primary source of income came from outside investment in the acquisition of user data. More than the standard emails, phone numbers, browsing behavior, and click-charts, they were trading in detailed analyses of the impulsive, premeditated, *and* guided decision-making processes of their millions of users. Plugged in, navigating their vast library of Original Experiences and user-generated content, his company could now map the reactions, decisions, even lingering emotional responses of anyone who stuck around long enough to let their imagination build on the preexisting foundation of an Original Experience—from what made a user blush to what made them cry out in pain or reject the virtual experience altogether. It was a deep well. More than what made people tick, they were beginning to understand what those ticks amounted to. The way a person *would* or *might* act. Even why.

While many of the company's partners were global advertising agencies and international corporations, they'd also attracted the attention of the organized branches of several major religions. Juggling those relationships—and keeping them hidden from one another—had been tricky from the start, and many of the deletions had in fact been part of an effort to assuage complaints from representatives of certain powerful groups, which, left unaddressed, might have threatened the sustainability of those partnerships.

Censorship was too narrow a word, but it was one that a less informed person might use. And if the users were able to outline even half of what the company was up to, they—Miles and the company—were fucked.

After reading a few dozen posts from this painfully observant user, Miles had stopped to wipe the sweat from his chin. He was running on pure cream at this point, and its satisfaction was quickly curdling into what he knew would be a blocky bowel movement, so he'd shut his laptop, ordered a car, and silently squirmed in his seat at the unfairness of his situation. These weren't his decisions. He was a lead creative with low-level management responsibilities. Not a censor. Not a true boss. He was in charge of generating content, or overseeing its generation, not assessing it or pulling it down. He wasn't the one sitting in boardrooms with representatives from the Church of Jesus Christ of Latter-Day Saints sorting out which experiences lived and which died. The problem was larger than he was. It contained him. He was as helpless as anyone else involved. But the more he'd read, the more he'd seen of his own name. His and Lily's, creative co-lead and senior designer on the project. Theirs were the public-facing names attached to *The Ghost Lover*—once the company's most popular, now the company's most widely denounced, experience. Which meant, should the revolution go full French, he and Lily would be among the first on the chopping block. Everyone knew who they were, but no one knew the men and women who'd actually determined the course of action being objected to.

Lily hadn't even wanted to work on *The Ghost Lover*. She'd called it "creepy as fuck, and more than a little dumb," but regrettably Miles had gone behind her back to have her assigned to the project.

He'd gotten away with it because early concepting showed *The Ghost Lover* could be done faster and cheaper, and would likely have a larger impact, than Lily's ongoing passion project—the hard-won and ambitious effort to design the company's first explicitly Cambodian OE. Based on her own life, it would require the user to navigate an experience as a Cambodian woman. This experience would be unique in that it allowed the user no opportunity to alter any aspect of the individual at the center of the experience, although other external elements were still subject to user manipulation.

Her stated goal had been to create the first OE that directly grappled with questions of perspective, identity, and cultural background, and while everyone had agreed that Lily's project was important, a direction the company should be planning to pursue, they also agreed the constraint of the experience would likely be unpopular when compared with the total freedom provided in their other offerings. And, while doing the right thing was important to the company, the company needed to exist in order for the right thing to be done. They argued that projects like *The Ghost Lover*, early user testing of which had shown reasonably promising numbers, would help the company gain enough ground to pursue good but less market-solvent ideas like Lily's. So Lily had been reassigned to *The Ghost Lover*, bumping the timeline for her project into the following year, delaying it a length of time Miles knew invariably killed unfinished projects by placing them beyond the reach of even the longest-held strategic visions at the company.

That was the nature of their world: things changed. The timeliness of a project was its lifeline. This was precisely why Miles had needed Lily in the first place, to get

The Ghost Lover right, fast. She was the best on the team, and his favorite to boot. He was certain they would do good work together, and they had. As a result, they had successfully, and unthinkingly, built a wall around the people who would otherwise have been fucked by all this online turmoil—inviting the fuckers to fuck them instead.

After all this time, Miles was finally beginning to understand why he was paid so well for what until now had felt like relatively innocuous work.

✦

Fucked. Miles unfurled a Tootsie Roll in the back seat of his bleachy rideshare and suffered its waxy resistance. If a single user had been able to piece together this much of the story without access to internal documents—if it was this clear, this visible to anyone with enough time on their hands—Miles, not to mention the small arm of the company associated with the execution of his vision, was fucked. Or, if they weren't yet fucked, the things they'd have to do to keep themselves from getting fucked were potentially worse than the things they'd done to set themselves up to get fucked in the first place.

Miles wormed the wrapper between two half-empty water bottles crammed into a compartment in the car door and glanced out the window with hopes of seeing the moon, or the stars, or some other nonthreatening fixture of the natural world that might ease him back into what was feeling like an increasingly naïve belief that he was a small part of a much larger whole, an infinite universe that was essentially indifferent to the particular work problems he faced on any given night, but instead of being greeted by the moon, or the stars, or the planets in their glory, Miles was confronted with the uninterrupted glow of a parade of countless youths hunched over laptops in bay windows (he pictured acrylic tabletops, granite tabletops, marble tabletops), all of them working later than he was, focusing harder than he had been able to, pushing beyond him in their pursuit of whatever new idea promised an escape from exactly what it was that they were doing to achieve it. They would be at it for the rest of the night, whereas Miles had become quickly overwhelmed by his realization of just how much the users knew about what the company had done—and how much of it they attributed to him—and after only three hours, he had left work much farther from an answer than he'd been when he'd started.

As he was diligently carted up the narrowing streets of his neighborhood, Miles felt helplessly exposed. If users could so easily stumble onto the company's darkest secrets, it would be no trouble at all to find out that Miles had two daughters. His whole life was online. His address. His surgical records. Documents evidencing the fact that, at his request, his parents had allowed him to get circumcised at thirteen, at a time when he was feeling particularly out of place at school. The comforts of digitization, the ease with which he could now access his own medical history, passwords, bank account information—it could all be turned against him like in some '90s hacker thriller.

What had made those horror stories of the nascent internet compelling yet palatable was the concession that the personal records of most unremarkable individuals—and until now Miles had considered himself one of these— weren't worth the outlay of time and attention necessary to acquire them. No one would care to. Not unless those individuals somehow accidentally, or by devious design, became the center of a larger ongoing scandal.

Like the youths in those bay windows, the company's horde of users never slept. They never tired. They were always humming, working in shifts, united in their dedication to the fickle cause of fucking Miles. If he was going to survive, he'd need a plan that went far beyond a retroactive code of conduct. And yet that's all he'd been ordered to provide.

WORKING LATE WON'T SAVE YOU

Miles put the threat with the others, pinning it under the dome of a glass paperweight in a low drawer by the sink. After failing to locate the first threat in the trash, he'd decided to keep the other threats where he could see them. Throwing them away felt too small—like he wasn't appropriately acknowledging the severity of the situation—but taking them to the authorities felt like he would be starting a countdown clock, forcing a climax that might otherwise still be avoided. Miles also worried that going to the police would confirm the claims of the harassment hotline's operator that there was nothing they could do for him, but only after he'd gone to the trouble of admitting he was afraid and in need of protection. If there was truly nothing to be done, he hoped to at least spare himself the humiliation.

Miles was spiraling. He took out his phone, reopened the rideshare app, and added twenty dollars to his initial tip. If there was nothing he could do, he could at least do something. And it did make him feel better, picturing the driver in his car, a bright alert sound dinging. Truthfully, Miles had no idea how the tipping component worked for this particular rideshare service, but an increased tip, whatever percentage of it was received by the driver, was an easy way of improving his mood, as it was safe to assume it improved the mood, however marginally, of the anonymous person who'd carted Miles from his office to his home without commenting on the amount of sweat soaking into his back seat—a thought that gave Miles the faintest shimmer of relief. It might not have been enough to tilt the cosmic scales in his direction, but tipping to excess did contribute in some small way to a moment of decreased suffering in the world—regardless of what came before it or what would come next—and that was a comfort Miles was glad he could access whenever he wished.

WORKING LATE WON'T SAVE YOU

It was too late for the company to deny what it had done, and too late to dissolve suspicions by trying to

explain away its behavior. Still, something had to be revealed. Something other than the truth. And whatever
that something was, it had to have the capacity to absorb
or redirect the call being sounded by the user horde. The
company itself would no doubt survive whatever happened, which meant it was on Miles to save himself. But
he'd arrived home with no plan other than to get out of
the path of the wave that was growing online. His only
instinct was to hide, though he had not moved from his
kitchen. He had not stopped staring at his phone.

Miles realized that, at some point in the last few seconds, he had been stilled by an idea, or by the feeling that
an idea would soon emerge. He felt its lingering electricity.
But when he reached for it again, the idea was gone. He
reviewed what he could of his recent thoughts: the threat,
the lawyer, the users, the youths. At a loss, he added another tip to his ride. Doing something. And, unexpectedly,
the feeling of a nascent idea washed over him once more,
like hot water added to a bath. The tip was it. The tip had
done it. The relief of the tip, he realized, had evoked that
electrical feeling, and again he felt the crowded mental
sensation of an idea without edges, slowly taking shape.
He had to be careful with it. He had to be delicate. The
more desperate he was to grasp the idea before it was fully
formed, the higher his chance of permanently scattering
its disparate pieces. The best thing he could do was stop
trying. He needed to surrender whatever incipient idea he
was having to that basement level of focus that seemed
to do most of the heavy lifting, put it out of his thoughts,

and trust that, with any luck, the idea would return, fully formed, on its own.

WORKING LATE WON'T SAVE YOU

The threat was right. Working late wouldn't save him. Miles suddenly knew that if he was going to survive these unsettling developments, he needed to surrender whatever idea his mind was struggling to form to that basement level of his consciousness that seemed to do most of the heavy lifting. He needed to focus on something else.

✦

"Girls," Miles said, pushing open the door to the living room with his right foot, "what do you say to—" He stopped.

His ten-year-old was seated on the floor at the center of the room, watching his six-year-old squirm.

She was tied to a decorative wicker bench, her arms extended straight over her head. In her mouth was a wad of mismatched socks.

"What is this?" he said.

His ten-year-old met his worried glance with a grin meant to calm him.

"She said she could get out of any knot," she said.

The rope she'd tied around his six-year-old's wrists and ankles ran under the armrests on either side of the bench, completing a loop behind its broad, straight back.

When his six-year-old moved her legs, the rope pulled at her arms. When she wriggled her wrists, it pulled at her legs. Her eyelids were red around the rims, from crying he guessed, though her eyes were dry and shut. She was focused on the rope, getting nowhere.

"Untie your sister," he said.

"You don't think she can do it?" said his ten-year-old. "You don't believe in her?"

"You're hurting her," he said. He could see where the ropes were abrading his six-year-old's wrists. Each movement provoked a wince. He crossed to her.

"Dad!" cried his ten-year-old. "You're ruining it!"

"Don't!" said his six-year-old as he pulled the socks from her mouth. "We're playing."

6

"The girls need a vacation," Miles told his wife.

"You're saving these?" She lifted the paperweight from the kitchen drawer and used the bottle opener on its opposite side to crack a twenty-two-ounce bottle of beer.

"I want to talk about the girls," he said.

"Right," she said. "Vacation." She emptied two-thirds of the bottle into a frosty glass from the freezer, adding to it as she sipped. "But, honestly," she said. "Why?"

Miles had gotten his daughters to bed after a protracted screaming fight. He had tried to reason with them but had eventually given up, letting them scream themselves out instead, before tucking them in. They'd been dead asleep for over an hour when his wife finally arrived home. All the evidence of what transpired had vanished, and there was no way for him to accurately describe what he'd been through without sounding dramatic, so he hadn't bothered to try. The cost of his wife not understanding, however, was that he was now finding it hard to keep her on topic.

"It doesn't feel right to throw them away," he said. "Maybe I'm not convinced they're nothing. Or if they are nothing, throwing them out doesn't feel necessary."

"You need to make up your mind," she said. She was facing away from him, staring at the wall behind the sink and steadily working her beer.

"Okay," he said. "How about Michigan? The lakes."

"Either these are serious threats," she continued, "and we are possibly in danger. Our *children* are possibly in danger. In which case, you need to hand them over to the police, and we need to strategize. Or they're not serious threats and saving them is a perverse form of vanity. Either way, they aren't holiday cards from old friends."

"I don't want to talk about the threats," he said.

"Then get them out of the kitchen," she said.

"When I got home today," he said, "Maya had Mia tied up to the bench. Hands over her head. Her wrists were bleeding."

"Shit," said his wife.

Finally, he had her.

She tilted the last of the beer into her glass, then forced the empty bottle into the recycling can and joined him at the table.

"I don't care where we go," he said. "I just want to be gone."

"I think you like it," she said.

"What?" he said.

"Getting death threats."

"Come on," he said.

"You like the attention," she said. "It makes you feel important. I don't blame you. I'm sure it's nice."

"Getting death threats is nice?"

"You know what I mean," she said.

"We could go to that place in Maine," he said. "The one from last year."

"I can't with the lobster," she said, slowly moving her gaze to random points in the room, as if she were following a fly.

Miles tried to track her focus, but there was no discernible pattern. It was like she'd left her body on autopilot while she worked out a tangle behind the wall of her skull.

"What is it?" he said.

"You're afraid to get rid of them," she said, "because it means more to be getting death threats than nothing at all." She licked her upper lip, first to get rid of the foam, then several more times for no apparent reason.

Miles studied her, struggling with how to proceed. Since she arrived, she'd been hijacking the conversation, looking for opportunities to turn it back on him and point out the ways in which his irrational and anxious response to a mounting issue would only serve to make things worse for his family—which was incredibly anxiety-inducing.

"You don't want to go," he said.

"I didn't say that," she said. She sipped again.

"You haven't said you want to," he said. "Or even that you would."

"I just feel like you're not telling me something," she said. "Why now?"

Miles felt the same way—she'd been acting strange since the beginning of the conversation—but he had no productive way of turning the question back on her at this point without sounding like a petulant child.

"You never responded to Michigan," he said.

"I said no to Michigan," she said.

"You didn't," he said.

"Well," she said. "No. I don't want to go to Michigan for vacation."

"Where do you want to go?" he said.

"You need a want, Miles," she said. "You brought it up, so you should know where we're going. I should be hearing why where you want to go is right."

"You don't want to be with someone like that," he said.

"Someone who knows what he wants?" she said. She gripped the glass, watching the foam recede into her last inch of beer.

"Wanting to go isn't a want?" he said.

She sat with that a moment before saying, "We'll go to Texas," as if they'd been discussing Texas as an option all along. "West Texas for two weeks."

"Texas." Miles sat back, pretending Texas wasn't a loaded proposition. As if there was nothing to say about it other than yes or no.

He was surprised at the suggestion, but he didn't want to call it out. The threat of collapsing the whole enterprise still hung in the air between them. It was better to retreat into whatever was being offered. He was getting what he'd asked for, after all.

"It'll be hot this time of year," he said, trying to sound casual.

"Hot," said his wife, "and dry."

Despite the fact that the girls hadn't been to Texas yet, or that Miles had never been to Texas with his wife, or that *hot* and *dry* made up a significant percentage of the few words his wife had ever chosen to say to him about Texas, her assertion that they would go there was the only surprise of the evening that had given Miles any hope. In truth, he found it oddly sweet that he'd come to his wife with concerns about their children, and she'd decided, for whatever reason, to finally share with them the place where she'd grown up. He was grateful for it, if a little uneasy.

"How are you?" he said.

"Fine," she said.

"Fine?" he said.

"Fine." She sipped. "Is there more to say if that's the case?"

"No," he said.

"Then okay," she said.

"Okay," he said. "We'll get a cabin by a creek in West Texas."

part two

the middle

7

Miles and his family flew into El Paso and drove east along the highway headed for a rustic cabin in the West Texas scrub. The girls had been mercifully easy the whole flight, and his wife had been quiet for the first half of the drive. Miles drove and did his best to enjoy the scenery, trying to move as little as possible so as to avoid drawing attention to himself. There was no telling how long the peace would last.

From what he'd seen so far, Texas was one big Texaco. Beautiful in a way that reminded him of barbed wire. Richard Serra, everywhere he looked—rusty, large, and looming. The whole state needed a polish. A good, deep scrub. At the same time, it felt like putting too much pressure on anything would wear it to dust.

"We came here as kids," said his wife, surprising Miles from the passenger's seat.

"Yeah?" he said. He recalibrated his expectations for the drive. Maybe they would talk. Maybe they would tell stories. He had no idea what being in Texas was going to do to his wife. "I can't believe it's still standing," he said.

"Not the cabin," she said. "I'm not that old.

"West Texas," she added after a bit of silent road had passed. "Somewhere in the hills, so Dad could hunt."

The relics of Miles's childhood were few and far between. Buildings razed, friends and family distant or dead. He'd only meant to acknowledge the rarity of being able to return to an unchanged spot of childhood significance, but explaining that presented too many opportunities for further missteps, so he let it go. His wife rarely volunteered information about her upbringing. Until now he hadn't known her father hunted, and he had no idea the two of them had traveled alone together to the far corners of West Texas. He did know about her cat, Celine, and her dog, Booker, both of whom had been alive for most of her life. He also knew she had an in-depth knowledge of goats from years of breeding and raising them for show, though she had not thought of her goats as pets. As she'd explained it to him, they were more like athletes in her care, and that relationship was very specific. There were professional expectations placed on a show animal that had to be met if it was going to succeed, a dynamic that would strain the more indulgent relationship one might have with a pet.

"It's close to the difference," she'd said, "between affection and professional admiration. You can love something even though it challenges you, or refuses to live up to your expectations, maybe even because it does—but my feelings for a goat had exclusively to do with its success rates and general usefulness."

She'd been a blue-ribbon hound. Miles knew this

because she'd brought a box of them with her when they first moved in together. In fact, the presence of that box was why she'd had to tell him about the goats in the first place. A box of blue ribbons, and the closet space it required, demanded some kind of explanation, though she'd made a valiant effort to avoid it.

While the goats had either succeeded or gotten the axe, and Booker and Celine had given witness to his wife's ongoing coming of age, Miles had been busy in Maryland, burying six dogs, four cats, and a pair of ducks—twelve pets in about seventeen years. He'd learned the death lesson early and hard, thanks to the dangerous, winding road he'd grown up on in rural Baltimore. The hole in his family's back fence had either kept breaking, as his parents had put forward, or they'd never fixed it well enough, or fixed it at all, as Miles had come to suspect. In either case, he admired his wife when she talked about her goats like she was reading from a manual, as well as when she talked about Booker like she was reading from a biography of the life of America's greatest dog. She knew how to care for things, as well as how to love them, but what impressed him the most was that she'd grown up knowing the difference.

"Birds," said his six-year-old from the back seat. She said it like she'd invented the word.

"Those are bats," said his ten-year-old.

"No," said his six-year-old.

"Look closer," said his ten-year-old. "You can't afford to be that stupid."

"Hey," said Miles. He glanced in the rearview mirror and saw a row of black birds lifting from a taut wire, like inverted flaps of skin.

"If you'd taken the highway," said his wife, "we'd be there."

"I wanted to see where you're from," he said.

"This isn't where I'm from," she said. "I told you. We came here when I was a kid."

Miles had wanted to take a scenic route, but the obvious side roads on the map went too far afield, adding hours to the drive or branching off into Northwest Texas, which his wife had said was more oil derricks and entertainment centers than idyllic rocks and rustic cabins. Curious as he was to see his first real Texan oil derrick, Miles also didn't want to risk getting lost or winding up in some random small town, measuring half the day in stop signs, so he'd tried to split the difference, settling for a narrow road on the map that seemed to dip away from the highway at times, but always returned within a half mile or so. Thirty minutes into the drive, he'd come to understand that the access road, as he'd learned it was called, was built for only and exactly that: accessing the highway. The view it offered was primarily off-ramps, gas stations, and uninspired graffiti on the occasional overpass. For the most part, Miles had the same view he would have had on the highway, only here he had to drive twenty miles per hour slower.

"But there are bats," he said.

"We're paying for a cabin," said his wife, "not vultures on an access road."

"So they *are* bats?" said his six-year-old, ignoring her mother.

"We don't know," said his wife. "We didn't see them. Talk to your sister."

"I saw them," said his ten-year-old. "They were bats."

"You don't know?" said his six-year-old, half ignoring her sister. "You didn't see?"

"That's right," said his wife. "It's one of life's great mysteries."

8

Five and a half hours later, they'd reached the cabin. Their grass-green Ford Taurus—the only full-sized rental left on the lot—was brilliant against the silty baked-out yellow of the cabin's actual lawn. Miles's wife hurried ahead with his daughters, while he stretched his legs in the yard, trying to find some secret joy hidden in the heat. Where there wasn't dead grass, the naked dirt was reddish brown and pocked with ant piles shaped like ziggurats. He blasted through them with the toe of his new boots, sending ants the size of Tylenol capsules arcing toward the porch. He watched them fan into the oily distance, spotting the only trees on the property, which were more like the skeletons of trees than actual trees. Leafless and thin, they staggered in a crooked line to the west, guided, Miles guessed, by the creek mentioned in the rental listing.

They'd only been here two minutes, but Miles could almost breathe again. He was very nearly happy. He lingered at the edge of the yard, watching the heat of the afternoon turn the air to grease, thinking it was one hundred percent pleasant how being somewhere new got you to notice new things.

✦

"I'd like to shoot that," said his ten-year-old, pointing at a rusty shotgun mounted over the cabin's stone fireplace.

"I don't think it works," said his wife. "It's all rusted."

"And it's a shotgun," Miles added. "So no."

"You don't tell me no," said his ten-year-old, slamming shut a massive iron sliding door and latching it from the other side, thereby claiming the master bedroom for herself.

"Nice," said his wife.

Miles was preparing to declare his firm resolve on the subject of firearms when it occurred to him that he had no idea how his wife felt about them. He knew now that her father was a hunter, at least a recreational hunter, which meant she'd grown up around guns. He wondered how much subtle Texan she'd managed to sneak by him over the years, how much about her she'd let him assume without bothering to correct him. He realized that, at this point, to declare firm resolve would be to swing blindly in the dark, hoping whatever contact he made was not fatal.

Before he could say anything more, Miles needed to talk to his wife about growing up with guns. He needed to know how she'd felt about them then and how she felt about them now. But these were the kinds of questions he'd learned to avoid. Harmless on the surface, there were accusations in their DNA. First, that his wife had been secretive and withholding of pertinent childhood information—which, however true, was a conversation that never ended well—and second, that some part of him worried she might have allowed their ten-year-old to remove a shotgun from its mount and wield it in the yard, if he hadn't been there to stop it.

As his family drained into the small rental cabin, Miles stood in its front room, trying not to look at the gun. He opened the rental app on his phone and messaged the owner of the cabin, letting them know his family had arrived safely and accessed the house without any trouble. He watched the flickering ellipsis of the owner's response for several seconds before adding:

ONE QUESTION . . .

CAN YOU ASSURE ME THE SHOTGUN
MOUNTED IN THE FRONT ROOM
ISN'T LOADED?

The owner's ellipsis vanished decisively, and the screen sat still. His question stared back at him unanswered, while Miles weighed his options. He could message again and push it further, potentially incurring the wrath of whoever sat anonymously on the other side of the line. Or he could wait and try to assume the best. Perhaps the cabin's owner was formulating an irritated but thorough response and had chosen to draft it longhand before typing it in. Or perhaps they were out at breakfast, searching for a socially appropriate time to become absorbed with messaging their short-term tenant through a rental app on their phone. Or perhaps they were in a historical hotel in New York City, this being one of several thousand rustic rentals they oversaw remotely, and they had just dropped their phone into the bubble-bathed basin of a large claw-foot tub. Miles didn't know. He couldn't know because the owner would not talk to him.

Miles's phone didn't buzz with a response until he'd lowered it, glancing once more at the shotgun mounted over the fireplace. He looked for signs of decrepitude, any discoloration that might somehow indicate to him the weapon's decommissioned status.

Other than a bit of rust, it looked clean. A little dusty, maybe. He had the phone clutched by his hip, and had nearly forgotten it, when it did, finally, buzz. Startled, Miles dropped the buzzing object in his hand, heard it clattering against the soft wood of the front room. But instead of bending to retrieve it, Miles found his attention was drawn by the awful sounds coming from outdoors. He hurried after them.

Miles would not read the owner's answer for several hours. He would not even think to. Outside, his six-year-old was screaming, filling the air with painful noise. He rushed to her, though she did not call for him. She did not call for her mother or her sister either. Outside, his six-year-old daughter was calling only for it, whatever *it* was, to stop.

9

From the porch, Miles watched his daughter roll in the dirt, slapping her face and legs. It almost looked like a game. When his ten-year-old was that age, she used to scream for help, but when Miles ran into the room, preparing to risk his life to save hers, he'd find her holding a doll facedown in the bathtub or a sink full of water, voicing the inanimate object's helpless cries.

"What is it?" Miles called to his six-year-old, struggling with the latch on the porch's screen door. He was hurrying but trying not to hurry so much that he would have more trouble with the latch than he already was. "I'm coming," he said.

The latch was a hook and a fish-eye bolt, which shouldn't have given him any trouble, but the two pieces were larger than he was used to, and they were rusted. They weren't yet rusted together, but they were coarse and hard to move. His strength was too much, or not enough, and his hands were trembling claws. His panic seemed to overload each of his other systems, which called into question the intelligence of the design behind the modern human, as his body invariably failed him whenever he needed it most.

"I'll be right there," he said, pushing and pinching, taking deep, long breaths to steady his hands, while trying to make each movement purposeful and productive. "I'm on my way."

His six-year-old wasn't responding to him or even looking in his direction. She was swiping at her arms and legs like her skin was on fire.

Ants. An endless line of marching red ants—maybe even some of the same ones he'd kicked—snaked their way to the grass from the raw red dirt by the porch. At the heart of their procession was a daughter-sized hole. His six-year-old was wriggling and rolling, collecting more of them from the line with each miscalculated movement. She knocked the ants away, but they kept coming.

"Stay still," he said, pointlessly. "Get up. I'm almost there."

With the hard knock of his knuckle against the underside of the latch, Miles tore loose a flap of skin and was finally able to pop the hook. The door swung open.

He ran a few steps, but the padding thud of rain slowed him. The incongruity of the sound was disorienting, and he looked up to confront the clear blue sky. His mouth hung open.

"Out of the way, Dad," said his ten-year-old. She was turning the far corner of the cabin, a coil of green hose wrapped around her shoulder. Water pushed into the dirt in gobs and spurts as she positioned her thumb over the hose's spout, directing the pressurized spray at her sister.

Miles watched his ten-year-old douse his six-year-old with water from the hose until she stopped slapping and screaming and started wailing instead. When her sister was clear, his ten-year-old redirected the spray onto the endless line of red ants, blasting them through the dirt, back up toward the screened-in porch.

It was okay, he thought, taking a breath, it was fine, that she was smiling.

"What happened?"

His wife was at the screen door now, watching the three of them from inside.

"Where were you?" he said.

"On the phone," she said.

"The phone?" he said.

"I was coming," she said.

"Were you coming," he said, "or were you on the phone?"

"I'm here now," she said.

✦

Miles's wife ran a bath and added cornstarch to the water, explaining that the mixture would soothe the itching and that a bath-full would be faster and easier than applying the paste to each bite. Miles took her word for it, stirring the curious mixture with a large decorative spoon he'd found mounted on a hook over the kitchen window, while his ten-year-old dragged chairs from the dining room table out the back door, down the steps, and into the dirt. A game, maybe. A game, he'd hoped.

"Does it hurt?" he asked his six-year-old, placing her in the chunky, warm bathwater.

"Yeah," she said, but she didn't cry or resist.

"Tilt," he said, once she was settled. She brought her head back so he could use a small bowl to pour the plaster-like mixture over the bites on her face and neck.

"Why do they bite like that?" she said.

He shrugged.

"Self-defense," he said. "Tilt."

His wife let out a small laugh from the toilet. She wiped, flushed, then joined him at the tub to take over with the mixing bowl. He was happy to move out of the way, back to the window, where he could try to get a look at what his ten-year-old was doing.

"But I was only looking," said his six-year-old. "I wanted to see where they were going."

"Ants don't have the cognitive capacity to distinguish between a threat and a friend," said his wife. "Do you understand?"

"Yeah," said his six-year-old.

Miles couldn't see his ten-year-old from the window in the bathroom, but he thought he could maybe hear her out there, dragging the chairs.

"Then what am I saying?" said his wife.

"I don't know," said his six-year-old, picking at dead ants in the bath.

"I'm saying some things can't be helped," she said. "Some creatures are more like the vacuum cleaner than you or me. They only know what they can do, and that isn't very much. You can't take it personally, because you're more complicated. They don't know what you know. You have to learn how to share the world with things that will never understand you. You have to account for that."

The dragging sounds from outside stopped, and a few seconds later Miles heard the faucet running in the kitchen.

"What do you think she's doing?" he said.

"I don't know," said his wife.

He wanted to investigate, but his six-year-old was staring at the bathwater. She was holding her face still, trying not to look any particular way, as if moving her face at all would cause the words to come spilling out of her mouth before she'd prepared them. These were rare moments, when his six-year-old was silenced by personal reflection. He wanted her to know it was okay. Whatever it was that was bothering her, he was there.

"What is it?" he said, crouching at the end of the claw-foot tub.

"Nothing," she said.

"All right," he said. "Why are you holding these?"

He pointed to the palmful of ants she'd collected from the water.

"Because I killed them," she said, looking down.

"That's all right," he said.

"I didn't mean to," she said.

"I know," he said.

"They were on me," she said.

"You didn't do anything," said his wife. "They rode you into the water and died. That's on them. Don't forget what happened out there."

"Here," said Miles. He held out both hands and took the ants from his six-year-old. "I'll bury them, okay?"

"The ants?" said his wife. "Where?"

"I don't know," he said, holding the puddle of dead ants in his cupped palms. "Out back, I guess."

10

I CAN TAKE IT AWAY

Miles stood in the empty kitchen, staring at the message from the cabin's owner. It did nothing to answer his question about the gun. Instead, it added another layer of discomfort to an already unpleasant situation—the potential arrival of the cabin's very human owner. Given the punctuation-free attitude of the message, it suddenly felt reasonable to assume the gun was loaded. But leaving a loaded gun in a rental cabin for all renters, regardless of their age, to encounter was such an irresponsible thing to do, Miles could not find it in his heart to believe it. His wife would have less trouble with it. She was not always generous in her estimations of people, but she'd also grown up around firearms, apparently, so who could say how she'd feel about this one? Whose side would she be on? Miles needed more information.

WOULD THAT BE NECESSARY?

He fired off his nudging response and watched the ellipsis flicker a bit, before surveying the room. The dining table sat naked, without its chairs. His six-year-old's new boots were piled by the front door in panic. Miles felt a twinge of pride at the sight.

The whole family had bought boots before they'd left. His right heel was already burning with a fresh blister just from driving out to the cabin. But the boots looked great. Buttery pleather. Hand-stitched. His wife and ten-year-old had gone for the real leather, and he could see in the folds and wrinkles already forming around their ankles the grimace of his cow friend from the farm two hours north of work. Even so, he hadn't objected. Not aloud. It was a family outing—they were all buying boots for Texas, so there was nothing to gain from making it all about him. Besides, his six-year-old had liked the look of the pleather more, which made him prouder than he had the words to describe. It might have been the pink dye or the rhinestone studs she was drawn to, but he liked to think it was the reverence for life inherent in the choice that had really moved her.

She'd called her pair "the most beautiful thing I ever saw." Miles agreed that it was.

OF COURSE NOT

The owner's response came late but firm, stripping Miles of his suspicion and replacing it with an acrid shame. He'd been rude, maybe. Curt. Too straightforward with the projections his paranoid mind had produced about the gun. It wasn't loaded. Of course it wasn't.

He put the phone away, glad he hadn't mentioned any of this to his wife. The issue could die here. In two weeks, the only other person who knew about it would be entirely out of his life forever. He could bury it.

Miles went to the back door and stepped onto the wooden ramp leading down to the yard, where he found the lines drawn into the dirt by the chair legs, but no daughter. No chairs.

He turned and stepped back into the cabin, where his wife waited for him in the kitchen. He heard the tub drain gurgling behind her.

"She's cold," said his wife. "She wants to start a fire."

"There's no wood," he said.

"I was hoping you'd get some," she said.

"I have the ants," he said. He saw a few small, wet footprints curving from the bathroom into the main room of the cabin.

"Still?" she said.

"Are we having a fight?" he said.

It came out like a burp. But if it was going to get asked, he was glad he'd managed to ask it before she did. If they were, that is. Having a fight.

"What do you mean?" she said.

"I don't know," he said.

"Then why did you ask it?" she said.

"I don't know," he said again, officially giving up any

advantage he'd gained by demonstrating he had no idea what to do with it.

"Well, then think about it," said his wife, "and get back to me."

11

Rather than make the twenty-minute drive into civiliza-
tion to buy firewood, Miles decided to tour the nearby
creek bed, looking for dry, fallen branches. A walk would
do him some good. He'd been taking more of them, or
trying to take more of them, ever since he'd overheard a
couple arguing the mental health benefits.

He'd been eating alone in an Indian restaurant—his
wife couldn't stand Indian food—when he'd overheard
the couple, two women, talking about walking as if they'd
been the ones to discover it.

"It balances the two sides of your brain," one said.

"And curbs your appetite," said the other.

There was a short pause, which made Miles worry
they'd caught him eavesdropping.

"I wish you wouldn't do that," said the first woman.

"Do what?" said the second.

"Turn every good thing into a punishment."

Miles thought of them as he slid on his boots, check-
ing the lining for stray ants and waiting to see if his wife
would feel suddenly and inexplicably compelled to call

him back and explain everything, or at least make an attempt at answering his question. He listened and heard nothing from inside the house, not even the sound of her leaving the room. So he gave up. He stepped out onto the porch, where only a damp, vestigial heat awaited him.

◆

Coming down off the porch—of course the latch worked liked a charm this time—Miles stopped to review the grisly ant holocaust. His ten-year-old had drowned hundreds of them, saving his six-year-old when he couldn't. When his wife seemingly wouldn't. The ant carcasses were huddled together, curled up along the edges of the now-dried-out canals his daughter had bored into the ground with pressure from the hose.

Something about the scene took the wind from him. Miles was struck with the sudden, palpable realization that the world was changing and, with it, his preparedness for the cost those changes would incur. Whatever was coming, he wasn't ready for it, though he'd always felt, abstractly, that he would be. But if he was being honest with himself, he had to admit that the events of that afternoon had proved he was anything but prepared. In fact, he seemed less prepared now than ever before. At least in the past he'd been able to operate a simple hook latch. Things were getting away from him, and it was possible that, from here on out, the most he would be able offer anyone would be an encouraging shout from behind a screen door.

As if in support of his new theory, Miles stood frozen in a scarred yard in Texas. His body seemed convinced that any step he took would only lead him to some awful and unpredictable fate.

YOU WILL BEG

The threat he'd received the day before they left had been broad but acutely menacing. Only three short words, it was surprising in its efficiency. Though it could be read as a vague promise, shallow hyperbole, it had given Miles the chilling feeling that whoever was sending the notes not only knew him but also knew him well. He would absolutely beg.

Strong as he sometimes thought he could be—mostly at work and mostly for no reason other than he'd spoken clearly and effectively on a subject he was about to put out of his mind—Miles knew the truth. When the time came, he wouldn't want to go. He would beg, and he would plead. And he would suffer.

Miles turned from the massacre to discover its architect. Deeper in the dark of the yard, his ten-year-old had brought together the seats of the four dining room chairs. She was lying across them, belly-down, using the far end of a long thick branch to tear at the heart of a ziggurat.

He approached her, noticing through the ankle-high grass that the legs of each chair were submerged in small containers of water. Mixing bowls, Tupperware, a rusted metal bucket. The corpses of each defensive wave of ants dotted the surface of the small pools, and his ten-year-old was pausing every now and then to plunge the business end of her tool into the bucket on her left, clearing it of any tiny heroes charging for the sunburned flesh of a vengeful god.

She had all but dissected the mound, scattering its superficial architecture to get at the tunnels beneath.

"What are you doing?" he said, eyeing the grass for any hidden squadrons of fire ants.

"Looking for the queen," she said.

"Why?" he said.

She stopped and cleared her ant-covered branch in the bucket once more.

"I'm going to find her," she said, "and I'm going to kill her. I'm going to break the ruthless hearts of her subjects and crush the spirit of the colony."

"Jesus," he said.

"Exactly," she said, plunging her stick into the desecrated mound. "With a sword."

✦

The scattered branches along the creek were as brittle as the grass in the yard. Miles gathered them, stacking them in his arms, and the bark chipped off in curled sleeves, like shaved chocolate. He knew he probably shouldn't have left his ten-year-old daughter alone with the ants, but it was unclear to him what he could have added to the scene. Even in her most concerning acts, she was admirably resourceful. Smart. Loyal. It was touching. Sure, there was something off about her, but increasingly with each year, and frankly for as far back as he could remember, there seemed to be something off about the world he'd brought her into. Seeing her with the hose, then so confidently splayed out on the dining room chairs, it was hard not to think of his daughter as more prepared for whatever was coming than he could ever be. Maybe the best thing he could do for her was to stay out of her way. She understood the laws of the land. She knew who she wanted to protect and how. Her clarity and capability in those areas alone suggested more internal resources than Miles could put to paper.

The closest Miles had come to serving some kind of greater good was working as a writers' assistant on a TV show for three years before his first daughter was born. By no means an original concept, the show had nevertheless been reviewed as an unrelenting critique of humanity's growing dependence on technology and was heralded as iconic. The *New York Times* had called its first season "deliciously depressing," while the *LA Times* had gone with "absolutely scathing in its depictions of the stranglehold tech has on domestic life." Though he hadn't written a word that wound up on air, Miles carried these quotes with him throughout his life like talismans, consulting them in times like these, when he was feeling particularly low, unaccomplished, or regretful.

Miles's theory as to what set their show apart from all the others like it was that the writing staff had made a point of writing without irony, treating their subjects with total sympathy and telling their stories from each character's unchallenged perspective. They wrote as if they sided with their characters in the struggle for something like alone time with their hearing aid's artificial intelligence, or in their quest to crowdsource an ideal father figure on an exclusively touch-based social media platform. It made the show more compelling that the critiques were never foregrounded but were subtly baked into the drama of each episode. Barely there at all. Their viewers, and there were millions of them, could end an episode satisfied, entertained, but with a strange charge they would recognize only later—after a few hours of sleep, when they woke suddenly and were unable to get back to bed—as depression. Midnight Mourning, die-hards had called it, but it was a phenomenon so widely and commonly experienced after watching the show that there'd been more than one academic paper published about it. There was even a popular online theory that the show's creators were somehow hypnotizing the audience, provoking these nightly existential crises as a part of some covert advertising campaign drummed up to sell digital sleep aids.

In truth, the intentions of the show's creators had been nothing but pure, at least at the start. All they'd set out to do was write a show that spoke to the part of their audience the writers felt was slowly dying, giving it cause to cry out in the middle of the night and make itself known. In one form or another, each writer on staff held the belief that living things preferred messy, unpredictable, visceral experiences over algorithmically derived satisfaction, however refined or efficient those itchy algorithms would become.

"There is no algorithm," one of the playwrights had written at the top of a dry-erase board set out for head-canoning, "for the wakeful human heart."

It was the most satisfying work Miles had ever done. But times change, and intentions rot.

When the show's numbers dropped after the first season, desperation crept in and the team had to admit it wasn't much of a stretch to, for example, start changing the smart ovens depicted on the show into brand-name smart ovens, at least the ones that hummed innocuously in the background of a given scene. After that, it wasn't long before the writers were hearing pitches from creative consultants with major advertising companies about which of their products would be the smartest, edgiest, yet most accessible ones to build a new episode around. They all agreed: the treatment of these products could still be critical, if necessary. Mildly satirical, at least. Funny, if that would suffice. They had permission to be as honest as they wanted to be, within the terms of a standard marketing contract.

These deals had kept the show afloat for a few more years, but with their skepticism rewarded, most of the audience seemed satisfied to turn their backs on the show long before the final episode aired. The reality of the situation provided a far better ending than anything the sellout writers would be allowed to come up with at this point. It was a tired, old story: another trusted perspective gone corporate, though there were fringe theories that the entire backslide had been orchestrated by the show's creators as part of a bleak meta-text meant to drive home the show's pessimistic perspective, placing the responsibility for confronting the future squarely on the shoulders of the now-awakened audience.

Even so, the final seasons of the show tanked, and it was quietly swept off the air, while everyone behind it continued to get rich, and everyone who'd loved it moved on to something new.

Ironically, it was the first season of that show that had brought the virtual reality company sniffing around in the first place. The show's creators had managed to evade the advances, but when the VR company circled back with offers for almost twice the salary of the average writing assistant, the creators had still passed, but had generously pointed the VR company in Miles's direction.

The show was finished—privately slated for cancellation after the completion of several ongoing advertising deals. Everyone who worked on it understood that, even without the obvious turn to corporate sponsorship, there were only so many ways they could make the case that we were doomed and it was all our fault before people stopped coming to them for their entertainment.

When the company's offer came through, right as the show was moving into its penultimate year and just after Miles's wife announced the imminent arrival of their second child, Miles had taken the new gig, reassuring himself that he would be able to find a way to do good at his new job as well. As a lead creative, he could directly influence the budding company's output, and he would have a hand in shaping user experience—far more influence than he'd come close to wielding on the show. He'd learn the ropes, manage what he could, and at the very least be able to afford substantial monthly donations to a few well-vetted and widely celebrated civil rights organizations while he sorted out his plans for how to begin going about more meaningful pursuits.

The truth, Miles realized—pushing the limits of how many birch branches he could carry without breaking them down into worthless pieces—was that life was a goddamn knot, ever tightening.

12

Miles walked along the creek's embankment, trying to ignore the quiet closing in on each of his crunching steps. As his eyes slowly adjusted to the dark, he could see the creek bed was dry. Judging from the state of the birch branches he carried, it hadn't held water in some time. He'd heard somewhere that there was only one naturally occurring lake in all of Texas, which spoke to the hardheaded and willful nature associated with the people of this state. People like his wife. If there were no lakes, she would dig however many were needed. If there was no rain, she would pull water from the sky.

Miles startled, not just at movement, but at movement without sound. In the trees ahead, there was a faint, white shuddering. He could not access his cell phone's light without losing the branches, and he worried that, if they fell, they would break apart like ash.

"Hello?" he said, after a moment of noisy shuffling.

"Sorry," came a voice from the dark.

Miles thought of running, but he could not locate the cabin on a mental map. He knew it was somewhere behind him. Somewhere nearby. Where, though, he wasn't certain, so if this was what he feared it could be, he knew he wouldn't make it.

"I was trying to stay out of your way," said the voice.

Miles was momentarily blinded. A white flash stole his vision, and in that moment, he could think of nothing to do but tighten every muscle in his body, press his teeth together, and wait.

"No one comes down here," said the voice. "Especially this time of night."

Miles opened his eyes to find a cone of white light articulating the dead leaves before him. The cone was born of a chunky yellow flashlight clutched by a red and cracking hand belonging to a gray-haired woman in flannels and dirt-stained Skechers.

"How is it?" she said.

She looked at him expectantly, while Miles mutely scrolled through a series of random scenarios from his past, searching for anything that might help him make sense of what was happening.

"The cabin," she said. "I'm the owner."

"Oh," he said, light with clarity. "Oh, we love it." He said it like he was gasping for air.

"Good," she said. "I'm glad to hear it."

"You live here?" he said.

"Nearby," she said. When she grinned, he could see the bulge of her tongue working her front teeth behind her upper lip. "We used to live here. But we're in the camper now."

"There's a camper?" he said.

"It's a ways," she said. "I guess I got in my head and wandered a bit too close. I don't mean to intrude. But maybe you need something while I'm out here? Towels? That kind of thing?"

"Oh," he said. "No. We're good on towels." Although, he realized, he had not checked.

"Old habits," she said, turning the flashlight in her hand. "You think you're wandering. Turns out you're circling."

"Right," he said. "Of course."

"Are you all right?" she said. "You're shaking."

Miles stuck out his right foot, and she adjusted the light to hold it. His pleather boot twitched in the air between them.

"I guess I am," he said. "I was surprised, is all."

She shifted the light again and he brought down his boot, wondering why the hell he would have done something like stick his leg out just then.

"I just didn't expect you," he said.

"Of course," she said. "But I wouldn't be scared out here. There's nothing for miles. Have your fire. Try and enjoy it." She gestured at the branches perched on his vibrating forearms.

"Right," he said. "Right. Of course."

There was an awkward silence between them and the woods. Miles wanted only to turn and walk away, but he was overcome with the urge to bridge the growing gap between them and find some feeling of closure before turning his back on a stranger in the dark.

"The gun," he said, like a burp.

"It's a flashlight," she said, grinning again.

"In the cabin, I mean." He shifted the branches. "I wrote you about it."

"The twelve-gauge?" She asked it like he was the one who'd stopped making sense. "I said I'd come get it."

"Okay, yeah," he said. "Yeah, if it's easy, sure."

Now that he'd met her, it seemed easier to have her over than to extricate himself from the conversation without feeling that he'd somehow offended her.

"It's no trouble," she said, easing into the gentle demeanor of a person tasked with hosting strangers. "I've been meaning to. But it was my dad's, and . . . it felt weird when it came time to bring it down and box it up, if you understand what I mean. We were figuring things out, and I just couldn't. It's funny. Of all the things, I couldn't bring myself to take a rusted shotgun off the wall. But I can. I will. I'll come by. I'm not saying that about it now, you understand. I'm just saying."

"Right," he said. "Yeah, sure. Come whenever." His nerves were making it hard to listen. He was being pulled in all directions by mounting anxious energy, and agreeing with what she said, though only half-aware of what it meant, seemed to be the only thing holding him in place.

"The cabin too," she added, spinning the flashlight again.

"Right," he said. "The cabin."

"It was his," she said. "Then it was ours." She twitched the light side to side, cutting its beam into ghosts between the trees. "Now it's yours."

She clicked off the light and clicked it on again. Miles's pupils protested, and he strained his face to fight the flinch.

"I'll come by in the morning if that's all right," she said. "It's getting late."

"Of course," he said. "Whenever it's easy."

"It's all easy." She dropped her grin and straight-up smiled.

Miles didn't know what to make of it. He didn't know what to think about how this strange, woodsy woman was making him feel. Did she frighten him, or was he just uncomfortable around strangers? He was out of his element, and still recovering from the fright of encountering an unknown person in the dead of night, so he could not honestly tell which of the two of them was the odd one.

"And thank you," he added.

"Don't mention it," she said. She waved her light and took two lumbering steps down the embankment leading to the leaf-laden bed of the dry creek, before stopping and turning back.

"It'll be all right," she said.

Miles stared back at her, genuinely uncertain which of his problems she was referring to.

"What's that?" he said, after she'd waited him out.

"It's only a shotgun," she said.

"You mean it isn't loaded," he said.

"I mean you should take it easy," she said.

He watched her light wade deeper into the trees, until it finally blinked out behind some distant beam of darkness. He shifted the branches in his arms, regathering his sense of where he was.

Seeing someone out here, however briefly, had left him feeling much more alone than before. He needed to get back to his family. The cabin was somewhere behind him. He could walk that way until it revealed itself to him.

✦

The chairs were still in the backyard when he arrived, but his ten-year-old was a ghost. Any lingering concerns Miles had about his experience with the rental owner evaporated when he discovered the scattered remains of the ant mound.

At the center of a squirming crater was the ant-covered branch, his daughter's sword sticking upright from the dirt like a chimney. The surviving ants were like static, crawling endlessly over one another, up and down the stick. He didn't need to investigate further to know what he'd find pinned at its far end.

His ten-year-old daughter had done it. She'd killed the queen and broken the hearts of her subjects. And, once they finally came to terms with just how deep into the earth his daughter had buried the business end of that immovable branch, the spirit of the colony would be crushed as well, just as she'd said.

Miles never felt like he had the appropriate amount of concern for his children. He had trouble with the idea of there being some normal way they were supposed to be, so he vacillated between admiring them, even in their more surprising and strange moments, and suddenly loathing them when he felt they'd taken things too far—which was typically when he was hurt by something they'd done or embarrassed by them in public. Moments like these made him wonder if he'd gone about the parenting project all wrong. Was it better to interfere in some calculated way when confronted with a scene like this? If so, how could he be certain he wouldn't actually make things worse?

Miles's father had loved to tell him he'd never wanted kids. The story was, Miles's mother had come to his father one night, sat him down on the beige carpet of their living room, and told him outright:

"I'm going to have kids. I'd like to have them with you. But if you're not interested, I'll need to start making plans that account for that."

His father hadn't known what to do with the ultimatum: lose his wife or raise kids he didn't want. Of course, he'd asked for time to think about it, but she'd made it clear that this wasn't a time to think. He was in, or he was out. So they'd had Miles. The path of least resistance. Come what inevitable resentments may. And surprisingly, at least as his father told the story, it had turned out fine. He even liked his son. They had fun.

"Truth is, the day I met you I knew you were going to be the most important thing in my life," his father liked to say. "I knew there was never going to be anything more meaningful to me than raising you. And I was right."

Miles's father had loved to tell the story and end it in

that way. Somehow, after everything they'd been through, the point was still that he'd been right.

His father told the story almost every time they saw each other. He told it to Miles's five-year-old a day after a stroke had paralyzed the left side of his body. Miles had come to tell his father about a new job he'd taken, designing virtual experiences he hoped could one day be used to enhance the quality of life for hospice patients. At least, that was an idea he'd had for a new application of the experiences he was designing, though it was failing to gain traction at the company. Instead of hearing him out, Miles's father had interrupted him to tell the story again, and Miles had sat silently by the window, soothing his agitation with a breathing technique he'd learned from a coworker who'd recently become obsessed with a new mindfulness podcast. Three weeks later, a blood clot in his father's leg broke free, traveling the length of an artery to his lungs before stopping his heart. Within a year, Miles was hard at work on *The Ghost Lover*.

Miles left the yard and headed for the cabin, trying to neutralize his expression while privately hoping he might die in some similarly unglamorous way. His father hadn't been at peace—there were still things he'd wanted to accomplish, and he would have left the hospital immediately if they'd let him—but he hadn't seemed afraid. At least, he hadn't acted afraid. He had simply, begrudgingly, gone. Death happened to Miles's father the same way Miles had. Against his will, but without detectable regret.

Miles hated his father's story. He always had. But

his reasons had evolved over time. Growing up, Miles resented the idea of his father being forced into parenthood, led by the threat of isolation into an unanticipated appreciation of his son. And perhaps as a consequence, Miles had rushed headlong into parenting, accepting its inevitability without a second thought. He hadn't felt his father's reticence, but he also hadn't accessed his father's epiphanic certainty.

Miles loved his daughters. He did. But at the same time, he had never been able to fully accept the idea that there would be nothing else in his life to look forward to. Nothing that could compete with things as they were right now, at this moment. But it wasn't as if he liked this about himself.

Miles knew he wasn't going to drop everything and chase after whatever unknown possibility might somehow mean more to him than his children, but that didn't mean the possibility didn't exist. By refusing to accept that there could be nothing more meaningful to him than raising his children, Miles believed he was allowing himself to imagine a future wherein his life would still have meaning should he one day find himself without them. It felt important, for himself, but also for his wife and his children, to maintain an outlook that left room for the possibility that whatever ultimately happened between them all in this long and unpredictable life, it wouldn't end him.

Miles mounted the stairs to the cabin's front porch, vowing not to let the growing distance between him and his daughters become permanent. They would drift, that was only natural, but he would be there for them when they came back, whether he wanted to be or not. At the very least, he wanted his daughters to be able to review the time they'd spent together and confidently say that their father had tried. And it didn't have to be the most meaningful thing in his life for him to do that.

13

"Mia," said Miles, spilling the branches onto the floor of the cabin, "did you see what your older sister did?"

The fire was roaring. His wife was seated in a rocking chair near the center of the room, and she glanced at the branches he'd dropped before shaking her head and pointing to a stack by the fire.

"There was a bin out back," she said. "What did she do?"

"Who?" said Miles. He heard Mia and Maya upstairs, thudding back and forth across the creaking wood.

"Maya," she said.

"Oh," he said. "It's a long story."

He delicately guided the fragile branches toward the stone hearth with the edge of his foot, then sat on the floor by the fireplace, gathering bits of broken bark from the branches and tossing them in.

"I saw the owner," he said.

"Are you scared of me?" said his wife.

Miles shifted uncomfortably, then shifted back. She was staring at him from the edge of the rocking chair, tilting it all the way forward like she could spill.

"Me?" he said.

"You," she said.

Instead of answering, he examined his forearms, which were covered in red dots where the wood had rested. They looked like insect bites, but they didn't itch. They felt hot. He imagined it could be from the fire, which was already singeing the long white hairs on his ears where his flesh curled in.

"What do you make of these?" he said, raising his arms to show his wife the bites.

"Answer me," she said.

"Scared of you," he said. He lowered his arms. "Why would you say that?"

"Because you keep showing up like you've got something to say," she said, "and when I ask you about it, you start in with this whole aw-shucks-who-me routine, like you never had a thought in the world."

"I do?" he said.

She laughed. Or scoffed. Or coughed. He was finding it hard to pay attention while her keen description of him nibbled at his ego.

"Is that laughter?" he said. He followed a squeaking sound coming from above them. It had to be Mia, squealing, pounding on the floor. For a moment, his wife watched the ceiling too, staring at it like she could see their daughters through the wood.

"Girls," she said, loud enough for them to hear her. Things went quiet.

On average, their daughters listened to her, and Miles

admired this as much as he couldn't understand it. Whatever she did, his wife always seemed to make sense to them. They treated her like a serious person. He wanted to know what that felt like, but it was another question he knew better than to ask.

"I've been thinking about the girls," he said, after a moment.

"Thinking what?" said his wife.

"I wonder sometimes if I should be doing more," he said, needlessly tossing one of his branches onto the fire. "Of course, I don't know what that would be."

"Miles," she said. "We've worked hard to get where we are. The girls are safe. Happy. I don't need you messing that up with a wonder. Just keep doing what you're doing, and don't smother your actual accomplishments with vague dissatisfaction."

"So you're saying I shouldn't quit my job?"

What he'd hoped would come out sounding like a joke came out whining and uncertain.

"Is that what we're talking about?" she said.

"No," he said. "Or I don't think so."

"Okay, well," she said, stopping the chair again with her foot, "when you say it like that, I start filling in blanks. I know it's not that you don't know, or don't think so; it's that you don't want to tell me what you actually think. Or you think you've already told me, and you're trying to make me work it out on my own. So. I start trying to think of things you might know but wouldn't want to say. I look at something like what you just asked, about quitting your job, the way you're letting it hang there in the air between us, and I start thinking things like maybe it's a threat. Like maybe you're saying that if I can't figure out some way to appease your chronic insecurity, you'll come home one afternoon with your tie all loosened and your job all gone. Is that what you're saying?"

"I'm saying," he said, "I don't know how much longer this job is going to exist. With or without my input."

"How could you not know?" she said.

He shrugged.

"Fuck that," she said. "Tell me."

In truth, he'd wanted to talk it through with her since the problem first came to his attention. His wife was an expert at coring the layers of Miles's anxiety for nuggets of relevant truth. She saw him faster than he could see himself, which was how she'd managed to be right from the start—he *was* scared of her—and also why he hadn't realized it until now.

Miles's parents had not been good communicators. Neither, he'd wager a guess, had his wife's. But as a child he'd observed that the worst eruptions between his parents occurred after days of silence. His house went from eerily quiet to explosive. To this day, he carried with him a vision of his mother spending a week without saying a word to his father before hurling an overstuffed garbage bag at his feet in the living room. The lingering smell of the burst bag had burned into Miles's subconscious like a brand.

As he grew older, Miles gravitated toward people who

opened themselves up to him early on, spilling their worries, shames, and insecurities like a chest of Legos for him to work with as he saw fit. When he'd met his wife, she was one of those people. She wasn't afraid to tell him how she felt or why. More than that, she didn't seem capable of hiding how she felt if she'd wanted to. She had such an expressive face; she didn't have to say a word half the time. Her long, large features revealed inner turmoil like a mood ring.

It wasn't until they'd been married for a year that he finally noticed her tendency to withdraw around the subject of her childhood. They'd had so many other things to talk about, at first. But after a while, he found he couldn't answer certain bank-security questions on her behalf. When her father died, and friends asked him how she was doing, he'd said she was okay, sad, but getting by. Months passed before he realized those were answers he'd come up with on his own, feelings he'd assumed a person would have, not feelings his wife had actually expressed. What she had actually done was shut down, withdraw, become quiet and reflective, bouncing problems or thoughts back at him like a mirror without ever revealing what was going on below the surface. She might have been okay. She might have been about to lose it. The truth was, Miles didn't know.

Once he'd seen that, it was hard to unsee. What had appeared to him as the shrewd management of a certain severity of mind—how quickly and aggressively his wife could make her disapproval or disinterest felt—was a distancing technique. When they were getting close to something she did not want to reveal or confront, she would lash out at him with disgust, denial, disapproval, or all three. Or she would simply make a meaningful face, and Miles would back down.

Realizing this—not all at once, but slowly over the years and with mounting resentment at how often he assumed he was being left in the dark—Miles had started to push her. Not literally, but if he caught her acting defensively, withholding details from her childhood, or avoiding conversations he thought it healthier for them to have—when she withdrew—Miles pursued. It was a bad strategy.

His pursuit and her further consequent withdrawal led to long, mean-spirited arguments that spiraled so far from the central question that neither of them could remember by the end what had been at stake or how a particular argument had started. When it was over, he only remembered, often shamefully, that his goal in pursuing the fight in the first place had been to make her feel comfortable opening up, the contradiction of which was never lost on him but was rarely taken to heart. He tended to focus instead on the regrettable split-second lizard-brain decisions he'd made, which it was going to take him months to outlive. The water he'd thrown the time she'd accused their relationship of *literally poisoning* her happiness. The time he'd admitted to reading her emails, believing then that she'd have no choice but to admit what he'd already inferred from conversation—that she was

more open with people she'd just met than with him—
so they could finally have that discussion. For close to a
year, they were miserable. Friends whispered and spec-
ulated. His wife admitted to crying in the shower. Desperate, Miles had eventually gone to a fortune-teller for
advice—or, he'd gone to a wine bar and had enough Côtes
du Rhône to dish out twenty dollars for advice from an
itinerant ex–grad student behind a cheap card table at
the back of the shop. Miles had described his problem
at length—giving surface descriptions of his and his
wife's most memorable confrontations, but moving on
before their regrettable conclusions—and the fortune-
teller had drawn several cards, carefully detailing their
various interpretations. When it was all starting to feel
very mushy, or the wine was finally wearing off, Miles
had pushed for a straight answer, and the fortune-teller
had given him one.

"Leave your wife alone," he'd said.

Miles had walked home annoyed, but he ultimately
took the fortune-teller's advice. And it worked. Sort of.
As soon as he backed off, he and his wife stopped arguing
all the time, at least with the same fervency. If pushing
her had pushed her away, leaving her alone—while not
bringing her as close as Miles would have liked—kept
the distance between them from fluctuating. Left to her
own designs, she held the line close enough to create an
atmosphere of intimacy, and to make many of her relevant
feelings known. On occasion, she even seemed to grow
comfortable enough to share things he knew she wouldn't

have if he'd pushed. So there was that. But in return there were years of her life he'd had to accept knowing nothing about, and portions of most days that went unaccounted for. That was the trade-off.

In the end, Miles had learned to accept that he'd married a private woman. It was one of life's uncomfortable ironies that he now supported their family by working for a company that traded in the voluntary erosion of personal privacy.

Miles stared at the fire, and his wife watched him try to work out a place to start. When he'd imagined this conversation, they were always at its midpoint. With no memory of how he'd started, Miles was somehow operating from a place of absolute clarity, explaining in articulate detail the situation he had waiting for him back at work. Inevitably, in the imagined conversation, his wife would interrupt him to reveal the obvious solution he'd been overlooking.

"Miles," she'd say, "it's clear what you need to do."

"Of course," he'd say. "Why didn't I think of that?"

Faced now with a request to fill the actual silence between them, Miles had no idea how to begin. After years of learning to be delicate with his wife around any topic she was slow to discuss, moments like these reminded him that she would be a terrible partner to herself. When she wanted information from him, he felt the pressure of that want like a subdermal zit.

"Miles," she said, letting him know with one word said flatly that this was a narrow window of opportunity.

"I don't know where to start," he said, starting with the truth.

"You just did it," she said. "Now don't stop."

Already, he felt better.

Though his wife would be a terrible partner to herself, Miles knew deep down that she was the perfect partner for someone like him. He was worried; she was prepared. Her expectation that he would get this right was low. All he needed to do was something, as all she wanted was some sense of what they were working with. She would build out from there on her own. He would start, she would listen, and they would eventually arrive at the truth.

For a moment, Miles forgot entirely about work, about the death threats, about his worry that he might one day stop loving his children. He stared at his wife, overwhelmed by feelings of love and appreciation for her. They moved through him like a breath of cold air, filling his eyes with water that seemed drawn directly from the insides of his cheeks. He loved her. He loved the way she could make him feel, which was little more than alive, but still fully alive, and fully present.

"I love you," he said, not stopping.

She freed her foot from the floor and started the rocker again.

"Don't," she said.

"Don't what?" he said.

"Do that," she said. "Just tell me what we're talking about."

"Sorry," he said, feeling more annoyed than apologetic at this point, but not wanting to derail things further.

Miles had hoped she would ask him why he'd said what he said, hoped she would invite him to describe that pure and positive feeling he'd been having for her in more detail. Then he could play the piano, or sing a libretto, or write it all down and hand it to her to read over and over again in private, swelling a little more each time with admiration for what he'd managed to express in just a few, well-chosen words. Or he could talk about work. He could try to describe a traveling anxiety, a growing darkness, the feeling that each part of his life was now narrowing to a lethal point.

"I'm sorry," he said again. "I'm trying to think."

"Don't think," she said.

"Okay," he said.

When Miles had pushed his wife in the past—conversationally, never physically—it hadn't been out of impatience or irritation with her silence (although he had sometimes felt those things). He'd pushed her because silence, in Miles's mind, was more dangerous than any problem that might result from actual conversation. Whatever the issue was, the best thing to do was to get it out and get it out early, before it could fester.

But Miles's wife was powerfully silent. He didn't know how to account for it. He would talk to her for minutes at a time, and, more often than not, he found whatever painful thing he'd gone to great lengths to describe would vanish completely in the face of her responding silence, or a single word said plainly. It was like breathing air into a net. Her silence filled the room with truths none of his carefully chosen words had even approached. Confronted with it, Miles was simply and precisely helpless, pulled underwater by a wave, with no choice but to let it roll him.

"You're still thinking," she said.

When she did speak, Miles's wife was careful. She was attentive to what she said, how she said it, and why, making her pauses more loaded, her half of the conversation more compelling, and her criticisms more devastating. Miles was messy by comparison, but he preferred to think of it as a strategy. It wasn't that he was incapable of getting it together; he was messy because carefulness in communication made him uneasy. It was too tactical, too close to dishonesty. It was a technique for people who were unwilling to confront the consequences of their true feelings. When Miles wasn't ready to reveal something, he'd made a practice of forcing himself anyway, at least when he could remember to, and he almost always felt better after doing so. Whatever the aftermath, he'd done what he could. The weight was lifted. *A burden shared is a burden halved.* Having it out beat holding it in.

If he'd resented his wife before, it wasn't because of the pressure she'd applied on him (which, conversely for him, was a source of relief). It was because she didn't respond the same way when he'd exerted similar pressure on her. Miles pushed her because he wanted to be pushed. He wanted her to want the same thing, because accepting that she might not want what he wanted, or feel how he felt, involved admitting that what he wanted or felt wasn't a given, wasn't a normal thing that any human could appreciate, but was instead particular to him. Even a little strange, maybe. Possibly pathological. And Miles didn't want to be strange or pathological. Miles wanted to be Miles.

"Miles," said his wife.

At best, they were a pair. They were both sides. They fit together in their capacity to fill in what the other could not. What he couldn't ask, she asked. What she didn't say, he said. Even if he was the only one getting anything out of all their desperate straining, it didn't change what she was asking of him.

"Go," said his wife.

So Miles went. He took a breath and told her everything. He told her about the deletions. About *The Ghost Lover*. The uproar, and the Church of Jesus Christ of Latter-Day Saints. He told her about his fear that he might one day stop loving their children. Once he'd started, it was hard to stop, because the more he talked, the better he felt. He carried on and spared no detail. In the face of this sudden and unexpected relief, Miles wanted to be thorough.

14

By the time Miles was describing a hastily thrown together after-hours meeting with the company's CEO and COO in the office's game room—during which he'd explained for the third time over kombuchas and Stella Artois that he'd done the research and determined that not only was a retroactive code of conduct something their angry users would see coming, it could potentially serve to unite the upset community further, as the groups they were dealing with, or at least the leaders of the groups they were dealing with, were smart, savvy, and on the lookout for general patterns of abuse of administrative power—his wife was on her back with her head in his lap, staring up at him with genuine affection.

He'd started with what he'd thought was bad news, explaining to her that, for him, Texas was no longer a vacation but a countdown to what would be either a public execution or a boldly disruptive pardon, and before he knew it, his wife had joined him on the rug by the fire.

He had no idea how it had happened, but he didn't want to jinx it. Miles recounted the story with his palms on the floor to either side of him, his fingers free of the stray strands of hair scattered across his wife's face. The more he talked, the smaller the cabin felt. He watched her stroke the hairless flesh of his forearm with her fingernails, and each new point of contact felt somehow inextricably linked to the words coming out of his mouth. So he kept talking. He told his wife more and more of what he'd said, exactly as he'd said it, recounting the unexpectedly magical combination of words that had somehow managed to bring all of this about—buying him time, two weeks, actually, and drawing his wife across the room through a simmering confrontation, straight into his lap, closer than they'd been outside of bed in months.

"The users," Miles said, quoting himself as he'd quoted himself to several bosses of increasing seniority only a few days before he and his family had left for the high Staked Plains of West Texas, "are perceptive and paranoid. They already think they know what we're up to, and the sudden appearance of a rickety code of conduct could be all the proof they need.

"Rather," he continued, trying not think, trying not to accidentally ruin this moment between the two of them with a poorly chosen phrase, "rather than reinforce the patterns our users detected on their own with a phony set of guidelines built from those observable patterns themselves, we, the company, have to break those patterns. We have to scramble the message, and do it in a way that puts the blame . . ."

He paused there, suddenly realizing that he wasn't

sure if this next part was something he wanted his wife to hear. It wasn't going to sound good—not if he said it as he'd said it to the people at work. But there was really no other way of saying it. Or none that occurred to him.

It wasn't that he became a different person at the office, but he changed his language to reflect different priorities from those he chose to emphasize at home. It was normal. It was something he'd grown used to and now did without thinking. Most of the time, this duality was fine. It was expected. There weren't a lot of opportunities for the two perspectives to appear at the same time, but somehow Miles had stumbled into such an opportunity.

In a last-second effort to save face, Miles made a twirling gesture with his hands. He spun his finger in the air, not wanting to say more, but hoping, on some level, that his wife already knew what he was going to say and would fill it in on her own. If he didn't actually say it, he could still deny it, depending on her reaction.

"On the users," she said, finishing the sentence exactly as he'd hoped. His wife was staring at the darkness above his right ear, her eyes catching the light of the fire in a way that made her look as if she could live forever.

"On the users," he agreed, watching her shift onto her side and press her ear to his thigh. "On them," he said again. "Not for moral lapses," he continued, "which would imply governing principles that might potentially be turned back on the company itself, but for *performance* issues, messaging that both aligns the users' goals with those of the company, and is, deep down, every millennial's secret weakness." He smiled, because this had gotten at least a chuckle in every other meeting.

But his wife gave only a quick nod, saying, "I don't think they're millennials. The people you're talking about."

"All right," he said, hurrying on. "My solution—my suggestion, I mean—was for the company to explain that the experiences weren't deleted because of the company's objections to their content; they were deleted because, in the lead-up to the unveiling of the next evolution of the virtual reality experience, the company needed to reclaim as much server space as possible. In preparation, we had to make hard, practical *business* decisions about what was essential to the platform and what was not. The deleted stories weren't deleted for content-related issues, but because the stories were underperforming. It was business. We couldn't justify keeping unpopular experiences afloat, at least for now. Maybe if those experiences had been attracting more users, or more repeat users, maybe if they had proved themselves indispensable, maybe *then* the company could have kept them on during the transition. But, as it stood, those experiences were like empty kayaks clogging a shipping channel. They had to be purged."

His wife was stroking his arm again.

"That's smart," she said.

Miles didn't know if it was smart, or easy, or if he had simply come up with an idea they were willing to try in order to buy themselves time, the potential failure of which could be easily pinned on him. It would be easy for them to cover their tracks and turn his mistake into another opportunity to make a new promise for a better future for the company.

"You think it's smart?" he said.

"Sure," she said. "If you figure it out."

"Right," he said.

"The next phase of premium virtual reality experiences," she said.

"Exactly," he said.

He wanted to kiss her. Miles wanted to kiss his wife, and he wanted to undress her, and he wanted there to be no cabin, no kids upstairs, just the fire and the rug and the two of them, Claire and Miles, the way they'd been when she was a woman working in wardrobe and he was an ill-advised mustache applying for a writer's assistant job.

"I have to come up with something that floats," he said, "or we're sunk."

The thumps from upstairs came to an abrupt stop, and Miles and his wife tilted their heads to listen. Silence was never a good sign.

"That's a bad attitude," she said.

He wondered if it was. He honestly wasn't sure if he knew how to tell the difference between when things were bad and when he was just thinking about them in an unproductive way. He knew he should be grateful for the confusion, but mostly he felt confused.

"Maybe," he said, "but it's the truth."

"You have something here most people don't get," she said. "Don't waste it feeling sorry for yourself."

He heard a scratching sound from above. It should

have been a relief, but it was soft and unnerving, like a mouse building a nest in the wall. He wished he had kissed her when he'd had the thought, because the moment was turning to mist, and the warmth between them was pushing up against the cool surface of an argument.

"Do you hear what I'm saying?" she said.

"I have something most people don't," he said, trying to forget the mouse. "A loving, supportive family," he added, hopefully.

His wife was no longer giving him a supportive look. She was looking at him like he was a tomato, like she could pop him with two fingers. He didn't know where moments like these came from. A few seconds ago, he'd felt good. He'd felt great. Now he felt split. He felt like something in his skin had turned, and it pained him just to look at her.

"No," she said. "That's not what I'm saying. I'm saying you have a chance. You have an opportunity. I don't think you understand how rare that is. You've got people listening to you. Pulling for you. They've given you time, resources, and more faith than you probably deserve. Get it right, and you, the company, me, and the girls, we'll all be better off. Maybe better than we've ever been. All you have to do is come up with a good idea."

Miles was distracted. He wanted his old feeling back. Even if she was right, he didn't like the way it felt. He tried doing what he'd done before, saying what was on his mind.

"What if I get it wrong?" he said. But the spell was broken.

"Don't," she said. She said it as if there were no other choice. As if they'd traveled all this way together only to arrive at this moment, when she might very well have to leave him.

He had a sulky sentence cued up, but a sound from upstairs put a pick between his ribs. Instinctively, he grabbed at his chest, at the organs hidden there. It was a scream, maybe. Or a split in the fabric of the desert—a small tear that ran through each layer of earth, straight to the center of suffering.

Somewhere, someone was hurt. His wife was up and climbing the stairs before he could realize how unhelpful he was being. Miles chased after her, navigating the darkness until they were together again, pounding at the locked door of his daughter's bedroom, demanding to be let in.

15

It was a couple of bruised ribs. Nothing broken, barely skin. But when the door popped open, they'd found his six-year-old pinned to the floor with the fire poker, held under the full weight of her sister, and she was signaling to them that she couldn't breathe.

Miles tried not to think about it on the drive home from urgent care, but he couldn't stop himself from imagining what might have happened if they hadn't managed to get the door open when they did. Worse, if he and his wife had gone for a walk, thinking the girls were asleep, or if they hadn't thought to check on them at all.

That was all her. His wife had bolted upstairs to save their daughter, while Miles had been preoccupied with visions of the end of the world. This was why there were two of them, he reasoned. This was why they were a team. You couldn't always be on top of everything, and there was always something coming.

✦

The next few days at the cabin were quiet, with no other incidents. But Miles and his wife were at a loss for what to do about what had happened. It didn't help that, immediately after the doctor had released them—assuring Miles there was no real harm done, only some mild bruising, painful, but nothing more than a few nights' discomfort— his ten-year-old had changed her tune. She'd gone from asking what she'd done, pretending like she didn't know, to plainly admitting her mistake. She claimed it was an accident. They'd been playing. She hadn't meant to hurt her and hadn't known what to do once she'd realized that she had.

His six-year-old confirmed it was a game.

"Maya was Maya," she said. "I was the queen."

For days, his ten-year-old tried acting like a perfect angel. She helped her sister with her ice packs. She helped cook, helped clean up. Well-intentioned as it all might have been, Miles couldn't shake the suspicion that she was doing it to keep her hands busy. Trying to prevent something worse from happening by making sure she always had a project. It was unsettling. Even if it was a game, his ten-year-old had pinned his six-year-old to the ground with the fire poker and held her there by the ribs.

"It tickled at first," said his six-year-old. "Then I squirmed because it tickled, and she had to push harder so I'd be still."

✦

"We could have you arrested," Miles told his ten-year-old, the night before they left.

He hadn't planned to say it, but no one was saying anything. No one had said anything for days. At least not about the incident. It was like his body had finally had enough and had decided to confront her with or without his approval.

"Miles," said his wife.

"For what?" said his ten-year-old.

"Assault," he said. "Attempted murder. Inciting mayhem."

"Nothing happened," said his ten-year-old.

"Stop," said his wife.

"We have to say something," he said.

His wife gave up on him and turned to their daughter. "You could have really hurt your sister," she said. "Do you understand that?"

"Yes," said his ten-year-old. "But it was a game. It wasn't supposed to hurt. That wasn't on purpose."

Miles couldn't help but wonder why she would have bothered pushing harder if it wasn't supposed to hurt. Where was the game in not stopping when that's what her sister was begging her to do?

It was cruelty. It was cruelty, plain and simple, and when his ten-year-old daughter had realized that would upset them, she'd changed her line. And that's what bothered him most. His daughter was aware of her own cruelty, and that's what she was trying to hide.

16

The night before they went home, Miles was visited by the Ghost Lover.

They were leaving first thing in the morning, but in the dream they were already back. Death threats had piled up under the mail slot. No one was collecting them. Miles sat in the hall, casually turning them over.

YOU CAN'T RUN

YOU CAN'T HIDE

YOU WILL BEG

DANCE

OR DIE

Four notes, selected at random, fell perfectly in order. He could hear his wife on the phone in the other room, using her taking-care-of-business voice. It was her most inviting tone, designed to gently usher the other party along and guide them toward a desired outcome. He admired it, the patience it took, and how successful she was with it. Refunded flights. The best camping spot in a ring of twenty. A fifty percent reduction on their monthly gas estimates. Miles was terrible on the phone, almost as bad as he was in the car, where he was always yelling at distracted drivers and inconsiderate pedestrians. He didn't like to think of himself as someone who was meaner when protected, but the evidence, he knew, suggested otherwise.

In the dream, the girls were at school, maybe. He had no idea what time it was. The light was all the same. Kind of blue. Kind of bright. He and his wife were almost never home alone together like this, but they were both occupied, so there was no opportunity to comment on it. She clearly had a project, and he was sitting in his pile of death threats. They each had a reason to be where they were. It was an unfamiliar feeling, but it was not unwelcome. He opened a few more.

NO SOUL. NO GHOST.

DEAD, DEAD. NOTHING MORE.

Somehow he knew they were all like this. Aggressively existential. He abandoned the pile to the hall. He had to pee anyway, and if he had no soul, and there was nothing waiting for him in the afterlife, he might as well use his body for what he could while he could and enjoy what few pleasures it had to offer along the way.

Miles found no toilet in the bathroom, only a tub that held a nude and hairless man.

"I'm looking for the toilet," said Miles.

The man gestured at the tub.

"I'm not peeing in there," said Miles.

"Climb in," said the man, "and you won't have to pee."

Oh, thought Miles. It's a dream.

He climbed into the tub with the man, sitting opposite him. Their legs tangled. As the man had promised, Miles no longer had to pee.

"You don't live here," said Miles. He leaned forward and felt the water running down his back in lines. He was trying to see the other man's face, which was somewhere in the air between them.

"I don't live," said the man.

"You're a ghost," said Miles.

"I'm Brian," said the ghost.

Miles leaned back, resting against the porcelain.

"Were you in my wall a few years ago?" he said.

"No," said Brian.

"Where's your face?" said Miles. He reached for Brian, but the distance between them grew to accommodate the presence of his hand.

"On a ski trip we took when you were twenty," said Brian. "We had our own secret language."

Miles sat with that a moment, letting the water go cold around him.

"You aren't my ghost, are you?" he said.

"I am," said Brian.

"Then what's my name?" said Miles.

"Maya," said the ghost.

17

Miles worked quietly in the dark. He got a fresh blanket from the trunk in the corner of the room and laid it over his wife, trying not to wake her. He bunched the blanket's edges, keeping them away from his side of the bed.

Slowly, he pulled up the old, soiled blanket. When it was clear of the mattress, he waited to see if she'd noticed anything. She didn't move, so he crossed to the other side of the bed and unhooked the bedsheet from his corner. Again, he took a step back. His side of the bed was now nude. A bold, golden stain had settled into the mattress like an inkblot, with only the one interpretation.

His wife lay bundled and sleeping beside the mess, dry and unaware. It was as much as he could hope for.

Miles opened a window nearby and quietly left the room.

✦

It wasn't the first time he'd peed himself in his sleep, but it was the first time a dream had tricked him. Normally, if he started peeing in a dream, he would wake up just as he was about to start peeing in real life and he would be able to stop himself, however painful it was, before making too big of a mess. This time, the pee had gone cold by the time he was up.

If it had to happen, though, he couldn't have picked a better night. They were leaving in a few hours. The cleaning crew would come in after them, and, assuming they were any good, they could deal with the smell. All he had to do was get through the morning, withstand a few hours of his wife's muted disgust, and then they would be headed home to forget all about it. His future would be built on accidents and small mercies.

✦

Miles took one of the chairs from the dinner table and set himself up in the dark out back. They'd spent almost two full weeks in the cabin, and he still hadn't sat down with his computer. His conversation with his wife had left him feeling much better, but he hadn't given any more thought to his work problem. Or, as his wife had called it, his work opportunity.

Wetting the bed had bought him time, though. He'd gone to sleep the night before trying to accept the fact that he had nothing. He was going to wake up in the morning, drive them several hours to the airport, and fly home empty-handed. Now he was up early, and he could sit in this chair until the sun rose. Whatever he had in front of him when it was time to go home, that's what he would bring with him.

✦

For an hour or two, Miles typed nonsense. Nonsense that would help no one. He told himself he was trying to shake something loose, but all he could think about was the dream. He understood the way dreams worked. You couldn't hold them accountable, carry them back into reality with you, and measure them against what you found there. But he couldn't let go of it all the same. Or it wouldn't let go of him. He was impressed with how little it had bothered him, being in a tub with someone else's ghost. It had been nice. Comfortable. He'd felt almost excited to be there, where everything was taken care of and the only expectation was that he let things go on as they were. His wife had a project in the other room, the person threatening his life was operating happily without his input, and he'd spent some time in the tub with a calm ghost who'd had the wrong address.

Miles stopped to make sure he was typing all this. He read it through, then read it again, stopping at the same place. Stopping at Brian. The dream was telling him something. Not about control, but about its absence. The checks of relationships.

In the distance, a shadow broke the light mounting the hill. Miles watched it settle there. A vaguely human shape, holding its size. The owner, maybe. She was wandering again. Or she'd finally come to retrieve the shotgun, which Miles had already moved to an insect-littered built-in above the cabinets in the kitchen. He hadn't known how to open it, how to check it, so he'd hidden it and hadn't thought about it again until this moment.

Miles wondered if the owner had come out here because she could smell the mess he'd made. Or perhaps she simply knew, her years in the house having forged some subconscious connection to it that granted her a supernatural awareness of when a guest had gone too far.

He could have worked a little harder to clean it up. This had been a person's home, after all. And her father's before her. He could have used the paper towels under the sink, or even a damp towel from the bathroom, the brief soiling of which he knew would be preferable to the permanent stain already settling into the surface of the mattress.

He was preparing to abandon his computer and go see what could be made of the mess inside when he noticed the shadow had vanished as quickly as it had appeared. The moment he was alone again, he forgave himself for the mattress. It wasn't his fault, after all—it was involuntary—and if she went so far as to mention it in a review, he could circle back with a statement about the potentially loaded shotgun she'd left on the premises, where his kids were at play. From the perspective of reputation management, he had the upper hand.

Miles watched the hill a moment before returning his attention to the computer in his lap.

Brian, he typed again.

He highlighted the name and underlined it.

Then Miles deleted everything he'd written before and wrote, *People.*

Other Brians.

18

"It took you two fucking weeks to come up with that?" said Lily.

They were downtown, surrounded by food trucks, and she was sitting on one of ten marble cubes decorating the edge of a giant chessboard, staring back at him in disbelief. It was his first Monday at the office since he'd left, and Miles was feeling uncharacteristically optimistic. He'd offered to buy lunch.

"It's an idea," he said.

"It's all idea," she said, stirring the mush in her cup with a bamboo spoon.

"But it could work," he said.

"It might work," she said. "Maybe, it could. Somehow. The point is, it's unlikely, given this is something you threw together last minute on a family vacation in Hicksville, Texas. Right now, it's a fucking fantasy. And all you can say is, 'It might work.' I mean, what if this ice cream solved the problem?"

All around them people in lanyards and button-downs tucked into jeans hollowed out their compostable food cartons, tossing them into trash bins or straight onto the ground.

"It's pitaya and activated charcoal," said Miles. "Not ice cream. My heart keeps having these hiccups. Palps."

"It's cold," she said. "It's covered in nuts and chocolate syrup. It's fucking ice cream. Shitty, health-flavored ice cream."

"I don't have anything else," he said. "This is the idea."

"Not having anything else doesn't make it an idea," she said. "You have no concept of what it will take to pull off something like this. The amount of time. The amount of money. The fucking blood, sweat, and tears. All for an idea that *might* work. People will get hired, and people will get fired. People will end up giving everything they have to this, and, in all likelihood, they'll wind up with nothing to show for it. Not because you tried and failed, but because you didn't put together a plan that accounts for the fact that human beings remain in the equation, regardless of how it pans out. You haven't thought it through beyond the possibility that it might buy us some time to sit around and find out what it looks like to try at this. You have an idea that *could* sound vaguely compelling to a small group of powerful people who are in desperate need of a compelling idea."

"But you have to admit," he said, "there's something to it. I did what they asked me to do. Not everyone can manage that much. Whatever comes next, it's not on me."

"Exactly," Lily sneered. "It falls to the rest of us." She scraped a layer of coconut shavings onto her spoon and tossed the rest of the bowl. "Miles," she said. "Do you understand the nature of my complaint?"

"Absolutely," he said, having only a vague idea that he did not.

"This will impact people you haven't considered in ways you haven't tried to imagine," she said.

"So tell me who and how," he said, "and I'll try to fix it. But in order for me to do that, we need something to keep us afloat, and this very well could be that something."

He took several steps in the direction of the office but turned back when he realized Lily was still at the cubes, watching him go.

"It will impact me," she said, calling for him from across the board.

Miles understood that people were complicated and unknowable creatures. He'd studied high modernism in college, and he'd once written a paper comparing *Swann's Way* to the poems in *The Palm at the End of the Mind*, so he understood that, abstractly, he was only talking to pieces of Lily that gestured at the larger, inaccessible whole. He also knew those pieces did more to obscure that larger Lily than they did to reveal the depths at which they hinted, despite whatever impression of her his senses joined with his imagination to conjure up. But he'd learned a few things since college as well. The longer he'd worked at the company, the easier it had become for him to see the ways in which large, unknowable wholes were also extremely predictable. However inaccessible the depths of Lily's true person might be, empirical evidence gathered over years of working together had revealed to Miles that the right formulation of self-degradation and personal praise would, inevitably, soften her edges. Though each time it felt to him like a naked manipulation—blatant, highly detectable, and underlined by each repetition—it had so far worked without fail. Whatever was being asked, no matter how much she objected to it, Lily tended to give in, provided Miles first admitted that he was helpless without her.

"*Us*," he said, stepping back from the cubes. "It will impact us."

She rolled her eyes, and he doubled down.

"We're teammates," he said. "We're partners. If you object this strongly, of course I'll reconsider. You have God-given gifts, and I'm just an idiot with half an idea. Don't think I don't know the truth."

"And what's that?" she said. She turned the ring on her thumb, a tell that signaled she was already reconsidering.

"Without you," he said, "I'm nothing."

"You're right," she said.

"Yeah?" he said.

"Yeah," she said. "You *do* need me. But God's got nothing to do with it."

"Of course," he said.

"And after I help?" she said.

"Exactly," he said. "*After*. If the idea takes, we'll have the time, resources, and the concentrated focus of an exciting new direction. We'll have our after. However stupid you may think it is, this idea could still provide us a future to plan for. Then, we get to talk about *after*."

Lily settled the ring.

"Fucking multiplayer," she said.

"Fungible reality," he corrected.

She raised her left hand and licked the air between her pointer and middle fingers.

"We put the fun in fungible," she said.

19

Within two hours, Miles had given his presentation and the company was officially changing direction. They'd wanted a solution; he'd given them a world.

The virtual reality experiences designed by the company, already shareable among individual users, would be modified to allow for simultaneous engagement. Multiple users would interact in, and with, the same experience at the same time. Together. Each would have the ongoing ability to modify the reality of the experience as they desired. Infinite sandboxes comprising one all-encompassing sandbox: the company's platform. It was the freedom the company had always promised, finally delivered.

The library of existing experiences—both OEs and user-generated content (UGC)—would be updated to continue serving as jumping-off points, just to get the users started. There would no doubt be a king-of-the-hill effect in the beginning, as users fought for dominance in a given experience and staked out their claims. But, Miles argued, they could bank on that effect leveling out.

As community social dynamics calcified, what started

as chaos would resolve into chaotic harmony. The checks of relationships. Other people. As they had with the arrival of the internet, then social media, users would group together, agreeing at least loosely upon the terms of a given reality, and they would thrive. After that, the users would work together to protect their preferred experiences, and the chaos would evolve into relative equilibrium. People would calm down. Or, if they didn't, it would be on them. There would still be biases guiding how the experiences were shaped, but users could no longer blame the company for those biases, as those biases would literally have emerged from the users themselves.

Or at least they would appear to. As Miles put it, the community's revolutionaries would be empowered to change their world as they saw fit, while the company's investors and religious partners would be able to quietly, or even aggressively, influence the experiences however and whenever they needed. The strength of the world's global religious leaders had always come from their ability to rally numbers and power around the promise of a certain central institution or organized system of thought. The next logical step of getting their followers to log on and influence a porous platform as instructed wasn't exactly a stretch. They could call it missionary work on the new frontier. As their armies swelled, so would the company's user accounts. In return, the company would sometimes be willing to tip the scales of battle, more quickly rendering certain changes to the experiences than others, if necessary. Only this time, they could be subtle about it.

It didn't solve all the company's problems, but it gave them a direction. It was something people could get excited about. Something to try. It bought them time. And, in the end, that meant money. A few more years on top. Even if it didn't work, people would pay into the idea that it might. Users and shareholders could be convinced, as it was an angle they hadn't tried, but it wasn't altogether new. It was a natural extension of what they'd already been trying to create, and it hadn't failed them yet.

✦

"It's still a fucking stupid idea," said Lily. She was standing with Miles under a cluster of golden balloon letters that spelled CONGRATULATINOS! It was the only place in the room where you couldn't read it.

"Maybe so," he said, "but it worked."

He tried to sip from his plastic flute of champagne, but the bubbles made him cough, and the cough made him hiccup.

"They're desperate," said Lily, "and you told them it would work. That's different."

Miles waggled his head, trying to breathe through the spasms.

"It gives"—he coughed—"it gives the users more power than they've ever had, which we're hoping will not only pacify those who are unhappy with the old model but also improve the overall experience for everyone on the platform."

"Bullshit," she said. "These are just things you're saying."

"I wish you were happier for us," he said.

"I'm happy for you," she said. But I don't see what this gets me." She finished her glass and grabbed another from a silver tray capping a waist-high speaker.

"It buys us both time," he said again.

"To find new fucking jobs," she said.

She grazed their coworkers with a look of disdain. The whole office was celebrating, though for most of them that meant nothing more than sitting by a slice of untouched sheet cake and a half-empty flute of champagne while continuing to work at their desks.

Miles joined her in scrutinizing their cohort, grateful for the conversational lull. While the room's open floor plan encouraged office-spanning surveys like the one they were using to fill their silence, Miles found that he only looked across the room like this when he was in situations like these: sizing up a bitter scene, hoping for the best possible outcome before some imminent plunge that would likely affect them all. He missed the old cubicles. He missed being able to hide. He spent most of his days now with his head tilted down, focusing on what was in front of him, afraid to look up out of fear of accidentally locking eyes with someone he wasn't prepared to talk to.

"You're kidding, right?" he said, after what felt like an appropriate amount of time to obscure the wave of mounting panic in his chest. "You wouldn't leave." He sipped, hoping it could end there but guessing that it wouldn't.

"If every crisis is a pivot," said Lily, "you know the shape you get, right?"

Miles ran his finger along the circular mouth of his empty champagne glass, doing his best to smirk away the question.

"A life preserver," he said.

"Right," said Lily, finishing her drink. "A big fucking zero."

20

Despite Lily's reservations, the announcement was a success.

In the years that followed, Miles's work life lurched forward and did not slow. Combined with a sleek new design for the company's proprietary headsets, the rollout brought in three hundred thousand new users in eight hours, all in anticipation of something the company had only promised to eventually deliver. All the old complaints remained, but factions splintered, and as daily activity increased, those voices represented a smaller and smaller percentage of the company's users, shifting from a central concern to a more easily delegated fringe issue.

Though installs waned as the company struggled to hold up its end of the deal, the numbers were still high above where they'd been when the announcement was made, which meant the announcement had served its purpose. It had bought them time.

It wasn't long before Miles found himself in a position he would never have anticipated, but to which he found he was oddly well-suited. Because he had no idea how to

realize his plan—product development wasn't his area—
Miles's day-to-day no longer carried even the faintest whiff
of creative work, which, he could finally be totally honest
with himself, had always challenged him and left him
with feelings of frustration and inadequacy. Now Miles
spent most of his time coordinating—and coordinating
with—the people who were actually equipped to deliver
on his ideas: scientists, experts, and engineers, as well as
the cracker-jack teams Lily had pulled together to execute
this massive undertaking. Complicated as Miles's new
work responsibilities could be, they now involved clear,
expressible goals. Most of the time, his job was simply
to determine which teams, or team members, were most
likely to achieve them. It was comparably easy work, and
he was much better at it than he'd ever been at anything
else in his life. Delegation, he found, suited him.

Still, Miles and Lily were busier than they'd ever
been, sometimes spending up to twenty-two hours in the
office, taking turns sleeping on the floor—though this
was strongly discouraged by the same mouths demanding
more results faster.

Lily, by all accounts, *crushed it*. She was the kind of
worker whose effectiveness increased in response to the
demands being placed on her. The more there was to do,
the more arms she seemed to grow. Miles couldn't have
been prouder. She was a laser, and he had pointed her.
Together, they were chopping the world to bits.

After eighteen months—only three more than
projected—they finally had something to present at a

company-wide meeting. Two weeks after that, the company announced a conference.

✦

"Being here," said one of the company's lead scientists before a crowd of thousands, "is the most astonishing event in a life that's had more than its share."

Doing his best to bend his face into the shape of a smile, the scientist went on to explain that what had started with users in headsets, sitting alone in their rooms, building fantasies on foundations designed for them by professionals like Miles and Lily—who did in fact receive the name-check—was about to evolve into a leading hub of virtual interconnectivity.

It was a bold claim, but if the company was able to deliver on even a small percentage of what it was promising, most people agreed it would be a profoundly robust platform. Sales skyrocketed, and while early users complained about the platform's mutability—experiences could change suddenly and without notice, as they were designed to be wrenched in new directions by any other user, at any time they desired—a quick look at the data revealed these complaints did not result in a rejection of the experiences. Overall retention rates increased by almost thirty percent, which meant the average user was lingering significantly longer than the company would have dared to hope for on the old platform. Users weren't just logging in for longer; they were responding to one another, rebuilding worlds they'd lost or exploring those that had taken their place. They were playing, fighting, critiquing, correcting, defending. *Sticky* was the word the company used in presentations. Like a web.

Even so, it wasn't long before smaller, edgier companies were nipping at their heels, and numbers that had once been cause for celebration quickly became the norm. Record-breaking statistics were no longer enough to keep the company afloat in a sea of competitors who now had a road map. At the same time, the company was rapidly approaching the limits of its hardware.

Convincing as their headsets could be, the experiences still weren't one hundred percent immersive, and while they'd made considerable investments of time and money developing the software necessary to execute on Miles's idea, their most aggressive competitors had been running alongside them, keeping pace by developing higher-quality hardware with more robust capabilities.

A key point of weakness in the company's current model was their dependency on available physical space for detail and depth in the VR experience. The more room users had for their setups, the better their experience of the platform would be. As the company grew in popularity, and their platform became more commonplace, this dependence on real-world locations was a growing source of frustration for users, as well as an area in which the company's competitors had the advantage. A few articles surfaced about the conversion of spare bedrooms, rooftop setups, and, in the Midwest, a long-defunct mall that had been gutted and converted into VR playgrounds, and that was all it took for the company's product to suddenly sound impractical rather than exciting. Too complicated, too burdensome, too niche. The image the company had hoped to establish of their headsets hung on the walls of every home around the world was quickly replaced with a top-down photo of a hollowed-out midwestern shopping mall, a dozen users confined to gridded cells, like a wasp's nest.

If that wasn't enough, there'd been fourteen major accidents—two deadly—within a year, not to mention the daily influx of requests (hundreds of thousands per day and climbing) from so-called satisfied users looking to expand, improve, and deepen their experience of the platform. The money was still pouring in, and new users were signing up every second, but it wasn't enough for the company to stay on top much longer, and on top was where they needed to be to continue operating at the level they currently were. Sliding from the top, or even close to from the top, meant losing money, users, and attention—signaling the death of the company to skittish investors. It had all happened so fast—they were still throwing parties for Miles!—but Miles was already starting to think success was something you could really only measure in degrees of dissatisfaction. Which wasn't to say dissatisfaction felt worse than failure—but life was quickly becoming less about the pursuit of good feeling, and more about deterring disappointment.

As the company's substantial lead in the field continued

to narrow, it was time again for a new direction. Miles and Lily were promoted to jobs with uncommunicative titles, earning gobs more money. They had all their old responsibilities but were now also tasked with dreaming up new ways the company might further distinguish itself. Their first order of business was the hardware problem, though it was an area neither of them knew very much about.

"Be creative," they were told. "Have fun with it."

Weeks of market research and user testing revealed that most users wanted more and less at the same time. More depth to the experiences, more detail and complexity, but a lower barrier to entry. Miles and Lily needed to use that information to produce an idea for something safer, simpler, and more satisfying than what their competitors could offer.

To be thorough, they'd had their team go through the company's archives, where they discovered that, in the early days, the company had explored the idea of self-contained units. At the time, cost and complexity had proved prohibitive. All Miles and Lily had to do was alert the company to the fact that these were no longer issues. Thanks to all they'd accomplished in the interim, their only winnowing resource at the moment was time.

Flush with cash and confident in the knowledge that brilliant minds the world over would leap at a chance to collaborate with them, Miles, Lily, and the team they oversaw put together a proposal for a stand-alone unit that could move and monitor a user's body for them, allowing the user to fully engage with the potential of the company's platform while remaining in an isolated, reclined, and passive state, safe from direct external interference.

For the purposes of the proposal, they'd called the unit the Egg.

✦

A popular history of the company would later report that in these days, "their capital was exceeded only by their luck." Not long after Miles and Lily birthed the idea of the Egg, the company struck gold a second time when they were approached by a medical hardware lab developing hyperresponsive casts for patients with paralyzed limbs. These were bionic sleeves that, when properly calibrated to the wearer, could reproduce the basic tasks of a functioning limb. In practice, they were crude but effective. For the company, it was the most promising technology they'd seen so far.

Instead of investing in the lab, as they were being asked to do, the company had swallowed it, purchasing its hardware, data, and research teams outright, and putting all of it to work on the development of a self-contained unit they could pair with their proprietary headsets. There was an initial protest purge, the result of which was a thirty percent loss of new employees, most of whom returned to the medical field. The company's executives referred to this period as "tailoring" (getting the fit right), and afterward Miles and Lily were returned to the software side of the company, leaving what was left of the lab's team to deliver on their concept.

Nearly a year of research, adaptation, and enormous expense led to a single, successful prototype: a self-contained pod that would someday, maybe, hopefully, be a fixture in the average person's living room. More important, the pod could do almost exactly what Miles and Lily had imagined. It could manipulate and respond to a user's whole body, all at once, in "perfect dystopian harmony," as Lily described it.

After the success of the first unit, they made two dozen more. Twenty were not-so-randomly distributed among beta testers, half of whom were directly or indirectly tied to investors; two went to executive leads on the project; and, to their surprise, Miles and Lily were each provided an Egg of their own.

The company talked about the Eggs as if they were being given to Miles and Lily as rewards for years of hard work, like exorbitantly expensive commemorative plaques, but the underlying message was that Miles and Lily would need to become intimately familiar with the new hardware's functionality so that they could start brainstorming ideas for the future of the company's OEs.

Arguably, OEs were no longer necessary, as their primary function could now be fulfilled by interactions among the users themselves. But as the landscape of the industry had shifted and grown, the company had discovered another source of potential value in the development of OEs as marketable IP.

Smaller companies with no hope of overtaking them were eager to exploit syndication rights, sequels, reboots, expanded worlds—anything to attach themselves to the bigger fish and cling for dear life. Unexpectedly, and via one of the most circuitous routes imaginable, the company had found itself in the larger, semi-legitimate entertainment studio position it had once hoped to hold. (A bit of discarded copy from the company's second profitable year had referred to them as "The Netflix of experience.") Fulfilling that early goal was by no means as promising as the company's overall direction, but the opportunity to accomplish it, and with a minimal outlay of resources, was enough for them to allocate some small percentage of employees to the execution of the necessary deals, giving the company an air of romanticism that might otherwise have been lost in the face of their recent large-scale pivots. This company, it seemed to argue, was not a company that abandoned dreams. They circled back. They closed the loop. They got it done.

As this flurry of activity came to an end, and the company settled comfortably onto the top of the pile once again—preparing themselves for the large-scale production of the Egg in coming years, which would usher in their inevitable market dominance—Miles and Lily were assigned to their old spots at their old desks, yet again tasked with figuring out what the company should do next.

Neighbors once more, Miles and Lily celebrated by facing each other and crossing their legs, each acting as if they were a mirror of the other. They laughed, pulled

faces, and finished a bottle of organic lager before returning to work.

Pages and pages of reports sat littered on the desks
before them, most of which were illegible to Miles, or
irrelevant to the tasks at hand. He was tired. He was
giddy. And given the volume of emails he received daily,
even crisp and freshly laser-printed paper communiqués
could easily take on the simple, white-noise quality of
clutter—ignorable obstacles to be pushed aside in pursuit
of quicker solutions to dire problems. It was easy to overlook a printout, one among thousands originally logged
by QA, printed and highlighted by an overly anxious
temp he'd never met, who would be gone in a few days
besides. Even easier, in fact, because the temp had folded
the printout and left it blank-side up, without a note.

part three

the end

21

YOUR WIFE AND DAUGHTERS WILL MOVE ON

Miles was smiling. For the first time in months, he was genuinely and extremely happy.

Things had become so hectic at work that Miles was giving less and less of his attention to the death threats. He collected them as they came—a week didn't pass without one—but the grip they'd once had on him had loosened, making room, as his wife had long ago suspected, for him to enjoy receiving them.

"What would you do," Miles said, "if my stalker broke into the house and killed me with a knife?"

"Stalker?" she said.

"Or whatever," he said.

He and his wife were drunk, nearly piled on the couch. No one was drinking anymore, but Miles and his wife loved to be drunk together, or they had a good time drunk together, which was becoming less and less the case while sober. Arguments still crept in, but the living room was a relative safe zone. The memories there were still good ones, and Miles was trying to enjoy them while he could.

His income had swelled after the launch of the new platform, the most tangible result of which was that the majority of his home had become unrecognizable to him. Thanks to his wife's efforts, the house was constantly under construction, and he no longer had any sense of how to distinguish between a temporary inconvenience and a new, permanent feature. Interior spaces wound through exteriors like a worm feasting on an apple, and mostly, when he walked the lengthy stone halls that connected one estranged room to the next, Miles tried to avoid looking up.

The only addition to the home that Miles felt had enhanced his life in any way was the new gate that had been installed in front of the house. Thick wood reinforced by a stainless steel frame, it was so imposing it reminded him of Scotland, of buildings older than the country in which he lived. It was thanks to the gate, or to the false sense of security that came with a sudden series of salary increases, that Miles's attitude toward the threats had started to change.

YOUR WIFE AND DAUGHTERS WILL
MOVE ON

YOU WILL VANISH, LIKE A MIGHTY
RIVER RUN DRY

They no longer held the urgency of a violent stranger at the door. In fact, Miles had come to see something perversely optimistic in the content of the new notes. If he had to go, at least no one would suffer. And if he was a river, at least he was mighty.

"I want to tell you something," said his wife.

"Answer the question," he said. "What would you do?"

"Fine," said his wife. She tilted her glass toward the carpet, watching the thin red lip of wine bulge at its rounded edge. "He just kills *you?*"

"He?" said Miles. He'd finished his drink and was eyeing the very narrow gap between her foot and his knee. He'd only need to shift an inch or two to close it.

"Statistically," she said.

"Okay," he said. "He only kills me."

"I'd leave for a few weeks," she said. "Pay someone to clean it up. Then move on."

"Come on," he said.

"I don't have a lot of years left," she said. "And two daughters to raise. Plus, you could have done something about the threats years ago, and you chose to ignore them. That's on you." She shifted herself upright, away from his knee. "My turn."

"You're forty-six," he said.

"A woman's sexual peak," she said, tapping her glass to make it sing.

"I don't believe you," he said. "I choose not to."

She set her hand in his, then lifted it to kiss his knuckle.

"It's true," she said. And then, as if to prove it, she said, "I was going to leave you in Texas."

He wasn't sure he'd heard her right. His hand went slack as he reexamined what she'd said, wishing he could diagram it like a sentence in English class—though he couldn't remember why or how that was done.

"Like an outlaw?" he said, blinking.

"Like a departure," she said. "A separation. My sister worked it out while we were planning the trip. I would propose a hike on the edge of Big Bend. Something you and the girls would be happy to avoid. Instead, I would drive toward New Mexico, and she would drive toward Texas, and we would meet halfway and drive back together. And . . ." Her voice cut out there. She moved her hand, encouraging him to take it, but he could only stare at it like an inanimate object that had suddenly come to life in his palm. He had no idea how to help it.

"Your sister?" he said.

"She didn't think I could do it alone," she said.

"Bullshit," he said.

"Calm down," she said. "I'm not leaving."

"But you wanted to," he said.

"I was going to," she said. "But I didn't. And I'm not."

"You're not," he said, "but you wanted to."

"Exactly," she said.

"But what happens next time?" he said. "Now that you've practiced?"

"You aren't listening," she said.

"I am," he said. "You're saying how quickly the winds can change. I'd better watch my step."

"No," she said. "I'm saying, I'd like to love you."

"But?" he said.

"But you're making it hard," she said.

Miles felt his skin sloughing off. His bones had quit too. He'd be nothing but a mess of hair and organs and blood after this, and she would like to love him.

"I think it's fair," he said, "to want to be able to live my life without feeling that I'm about to lose you to a grocery trip."

"A hike," she said.

"And you wanted me to know all this for what?" he said. "You wanted to leave, and now you're not, and you'd like to love me, and you wanted me to carry all this around with me for the rest of my life, for what?"

"This is what you asked for," she said.

"This is not what I asked for," he said.

"It's what you ask for all the time," she said.

"What do I ask for?" he said.

"How I feel," she said. "You ask me to tell you. So, this is how I felt."

"Well, shit," he said. "It's a little late."

The sympathy in her face evaporated, leaving only a pair of rolling eyes, and in that moment Miles saw his wife again. The animal in his palm became a hand—her hand—and he clutched it.

"Okay," he said. "Fine. You said it."

"What did I say?" she said.

"You'd like to love me," he said.

"That's not it," she said.

"That's exactly what you said," he said. "I heard it."

"But what I meant," she said, "what I'm *saying* is that I hope you can appreciate it."

"Appreciate what?" he said.

"What you asked for," she said. "How I feel."

"Okay," he said, considering only then how he felt about what she'd said. "Okay, I appreciate it."

"Appreciate what?" she said.

"I appreciate what you're saying," he said.

Miles could see in her face that none of these were the right words, or if they were the right words, they were the right words said the wrong way. He felt confused, as if the night had tricked him. He'd been lied to by wine, and he felt angrier about it than he wanted to feel.

Miles watched his wife start to speak, then stop herself, and in that silent moment they both understood that if she could accept what he was saying right now, as he'd said it, if she could take it at face value, she would at least be allowing herself the hope that he might be the kind of person who *wanted* to do the thing he was describing, who wanted to appreciate how she felt, and perhaps the best option was to leave it there, even if the opportunity for that hope was all that was really on offer.

"Okay, Miles," she said, pumping his hand once to let it go. "Okay, thank you."

22

Later that night, Miles was crouched on the floor of his office by the Egg, listening to another young operator tell him his feelings were natural. Valid. They would come and go. All he could do was accept what was happening to him and get on with his life. But that was exactly what Miles had been doing, and it had led him here.

"For some people, happiness will always be tangled up with thoughts about the inevitability of its end," said the operator. "These are valid feelings to have in response to what is happening in your life."

The phone was hot against his ear. He'd been at this for too many hours, but his thoughts were still half in conversation with his wife. He'd let her fall asleep, or start pretending, then immediately slid out from under the covers. He'd turned circles in his office on the phone, trying to keep his voice down, until the sun was rising and his ear was on fire.

"Some days will be easier," she said. "Some days you'll think only of the birds outside, bathing in the dog's water. But you're going to have hard days too. The choice is yours if you would let them stop you.

"Hello?" she said, after he'd gone several seconds without speaking.

"I'm here," he said, fingering the Egg behind him.

"And the notes," she said, "are still arriving?"

"Whose notes?" he said.

"You don't remember," she said. She sounded almost disappointed.

Miles tried to let himself have the thought, but the likelihood of it was so close to zero it was hard for him to hold it for very long. The odds were astronomical to begin with, and these hotlines were supposed to be designed to keep exactly this from happening. But, then again, nothing in his life was as it should be, so why wouldn't this one small thing fit the pattern?

"Right," he said. "Right. We spoke before."

"I shouldn't have said anything," she said. "This really isn't supposed to happen."

"And yet," he said, acting as if nothing could surprise him. After all, she didn't know him. She couldn't hold him against himself. That fact in and of itself seemed to give him permission to try at being someone different.

"And yet," she said.

"When did you know it was me?" he said.

"Your voice," she said. "I recognized it almost immediately."

"You did?" he said.

"Yeah," she said. "It's like a turtle."

"A turtle?" he said.

"I think about that call all the time," she said, moving past it.

"I didn't realize I'd called the abuse hotline," he said. "I meant to call for . . . I don't know, general therapy. Why do you still think about that call?"

"You did call for a therapeutic consultation," she said. "That's what this is. I'm not volunteering anymore. This is my job."

"Congratulatinos," he said.

"I'm sorry?" she said.

"It's a joke," he said. "It doesn't matter."

He set his back to the Egg and was surprised to find that it was warm.

"But it fits, you know?" she said.

"How's that?" he said. He couldn't stop wondering what exactly a turtle sounded like.

"Strange things have been happening to me all month," she said. "Someone stole my truck. Two days later it showed up again, abandoned in my neighbor's garage."

"Maybe they were trying to return it," he said.

"That's what the cop said," she said.

The warmth of the Egg encouraged Miles to settle in farther, and he sank down, rolling his head against its shell. It was almost soft. It seemed to give, embracing the curve of his skull without sacrificing support. He still hadn't been inside. Not once. He hadn't even turned it on, so he assumed its warmth was the result of some kind of automated maintenance. It only occurred to Miles from time to time—and now was one of those times—that he had no idea how the Egg worked. He'd had an idea, and the world had produced it. In that sense, it was a miracle. He was a conjurer. A humble demigod. He knew he could trust it, but he didn't.

"I don't know why," she said.

"Why what?" he said.

"Why I think about it," she said. "I guess it surprised me."

"The situation?" he said. "Or me? Or the turtle?"

"No," she said.

"Then what?" he said.

"I shouldn't say," she said. "This shouldn't be happening."

"So I shouldn't ask?"

"You seemed . . ."

She stopped, and Miles was struck with the overwhelming urge to keep her from saying any more about how he seemed.

"I used to work on a show," he said. But by the time he was approaching the end of his sentence, she had already started to talk.

"It made me feel like my job was worth doing," she said. "And like I was all right at it."

"You are all right at it," he said.

"Thank you," she said.

"Well, hang on a minute," he said, remembering the turtle. "That was that job. This is something different. If that's the case, I need time to assess your performance in this new area before I can speak to it."

"Have you considered regular appointments," she said, "with someone you could get to know?"

"Huh?" he said.

"A therapist," she said. "Regular appointments with a therapist who knows you."

"I tried," he said. "I didn't like him. Plus, you know me."

"What didn't you like?" She coughed. "I'm asking too much."

"I don't think he understood me," said Miles. "The last one, I mean."

"You saw more than one?" she said.

"I saw enough," he said. "This is better."

"Okay," she said. "All right. Then are you ready to be impressed?"

"You've got something better than the turtle comment?" he said.

"The very fact that this conversation is taking place illustrates the point I've been trying to make to you this whole time," she said. "Since we first spoke."

She was starting to sound more excited than confident, which made Miles uneasy.

"The sheer unpredictability of it, is what I'm saying," she said. "When something frightens us, and we're not used to being frightened, it's easy to imagine nothing but worst-case scenarios. The fact that the vast majority of death threats are never acted on, or even written with genuine intent, that doesn't influence us as much as the presence of the threat itself. For someone like you, a note like that makes a confrontation feel inevitable, and that is frightening. But the reality is, we have no idea what's going to happen to us from one day to the next. One call to the next. We map out our lives, set our intentions, aim our arrows, and all the while life keeps spinning its chaotic wheel. Which is why I always say, in most situations, the best thing to do is to wait and see. Focus on your daily life. Try not to let the anxiety of the moment take over. Because anxiety is not a predictive force. Whatever you know, or think you know, you still have no idea what's coming. So. There. Are you impressed?"

They sat together for several moments in erotic silence. At least Miles found it erotic. He pictured her with tattoos, which made him think of those piercings that go straight through your face and rest—he didn't know for certain—against your teeth? He searched his conversational protocol for a way to politely get off the phone. He didn't want to be a turtle thinking about a piercing pressed against this young woman's teeth.

"I have to go," he said. "My kids."

"Of course," she said. "We're always here."

◆

Miles ended the call and set his phone on the floor. The hotline hadn't helped. If anything, he felt stranger, more at odds with himself, like life was too chaotic to control. He knew it wasn't. Or he knew enough to know there was little profit to be gained from admitting that it was. Miles stood to take in the Egg. He'd been seated beside it half the night, but he had not yet turned to face it.

The company had wanted the Egg to feel inevitable, like the future had finally arrived, and it was the Egg. To achieve that effect, they'd based its design on concepts they'd stolen from popular science-fiction films, so it would look both known and newly realized. It shouldn't have creeped him out, but it did. It was roughly the size of a two-seater smart car. It looked casual, but inside it was lined with an array of sensors and sleeves. He'd seen the pieces separately but never together. He knew dozens of people who'd used them, thousands who'd worked to make the Egg safe, but when the lid finally did as it was programmed to do, lifting from its base without a sound, Miles felt like an animal had opened its jaws. The Egg's red, ribbed seat held his eye like a tongue. He couldn't look away. People did this all the time. Two dozen beta testers, soon to be thousands. Soon to be the world. Lily even. Lily, maybe. Infinity was waiting, and it was normal. Or it was going to be normal. Thanks to the Egg's rigid safety protocols, Miles knew he would not be trapped. He couldn't be. They'd made it safe. They'd had a job to do, and they'd done it. And if that was the case, the Egg could be all they'd ever said it was. It could be all he could think to want.

Stepping forward, Miles took two long, intentional looks at several small pieces of the world as he knew it. He looked at his wooden desk drawer with the loose knob he'd been meaning to fix, then at the morning-blue backyard visible through his new floor-to-ceiling windows. He felt superstitious, like he had to carry the protection of these distinct slivers of reality with him into the unknown, or risk losing them forever.

✦

The moment Miles sat down in the Egg, its sensors snapped into place around him. He watched the jaws of the machine come together as the sleeves slid over his thighs, his calves, and—once he'd been settled farther into the seat by their weight—his arms and neck.

There was no opportunity for darkness. The jaws of the Egg clamped shut, and Miles's vision flooded with invitations. Seductively half-realized, the library of experiences appeared before him like memories of a dream— visions of disparate stories accessible to him with the mere intention of a thought. The data suggested that most users had no trouble navigating the latest iteration of the library, but Miles wasn't sure how to proceed. Though they had been crafted by experts working at the tops of their fields, all of whom had been overseen by Miles, the choices available to him still somehow managed to feel like thoughts that were just out of reach, or voices heard through a wall. Somehow, the mix of familiar fragments with novel propositions was further disorienting to him, though the goal had been to smooth the onboarding process and narrow the gap between platforms. To that end, the Egg's library was preloaded with upgraded versions of old OEs and UGC, as well as a handful of all-new OEs they hoped would satisfy the first wave of users, or at least give them something to do until the Egg caught on. Miles tried not to look directly at *The Ghost Lover*, fearing the machine would misinterpret the look for an intention and thrust him into the heart of an unwanted experience.

The Ghost Lover had been fully upgraded to exploit the capabilities of the new hardware, and though it was technically done under Miles's supervision, he'd avoided any direct involvement with the upgrade. Partly because he was busy with all his other responsibilities, but mostly because he was ashamed of *The Ghost Lover* after all that had happened, and he felt any association with it acknowledged by him might one day be used against him.

He looked away and tried instead to feel pride for all they had accomplished. The library's design—a grid of three-dimensional icons that visibly rearranged itself as a user's focus shifted—was intentionally retrograde, but it still felt impressively alien to him. Until the machines were advanced enough to accurately preempt a user's decisions, the company wanted to re-create something that would remind users of shopping online or sifting through a box of used vinyl. For Miles, it reminded him of scanning the wall of videotapes at a rental store in Baltimore, only now the titles moved according to his inclination, and he was on the cover of all of them.

Not knowing exactly what he wanted, only what he didn't want, Miles scrolled through the preloads, searching for something unpopular enough to be empty. His team had gone back and forth on whether to share the number of users populating each experience at a given time. They'd ultimately decided against it, feeling pre-knowledge of the presence of others would cloud a user's ability to accept the experience at face value, as it would invite the question of whether certain details were being generated by oneself or someone else too early. Users, the company believed, needed to be able to see the reality of the experience as their own before they could accept the idea of its being shared, and shifted, by someone else. That feeling of being in control, however short-lived, both invested the user in the experience and helped ease them into accepting the reality that they were not.

So, for now, users went in blind. There was nothing to suggest anyone else would be with you in an experience when you first selected it—though if things went according to plan, there almost always certainly would be.

Eager to spend his first session alone, at least to start, Miles searched for old experiences that had fallen out of favor, ones that lacked the salacious urgency of popular teen fare like *My Monster and Me*, or more explicitly adult content like *On the Seventh Day, He Fed Me*. After several minutes of scrolling, Miles stumbled upon a Test Drive.

For months, users on the old platform had been obsessed with building experiences that involved nothing more than taking a certain type of car out for a spin in a suburban neighborhood, or on a long empty highway, or in a traffic jam. Miles had no idea why they'd been so popular, and no idea why their numbers tanked the moment the company started developing similar experiences in-house. All the time and money the company spent tracking the decision-making processes of almost a billion people to date, and some trends were still a total mystery to them. Seemingly rootless, they appeared as if from nowhere but were met with a degree of popularity that granted them the retroactive quality of having been inevitable. It was irritating. Well-paid company analysts were constantly speculating, proposing, guessing, but in the end they were almost never able to accurately predict the ideas their users would glom on to, or where things were headed from there. They could only really see where they'd come from, never where they were going—though a considerable portion of the company's income came from their being able to convince people that they could.

Before Miles's irritation could resolve into intention, he found himself seated in a Ford Taurus placed on a rural road outside Baltimore, where he'd spent most of his free time when he was a teenager. He accepted the road as it came to him, and drove in several long loops, turning off the snicker-worthy Cox Drive onto the more actionable High Street, all the while listening to a tape of his high school band, the Meatheads. One word. They were horrible, but, hearing it, he could remember the feeling of his unnecessarily fat guitar pick. A little glob of hard plastic. He remembered the blue tight-pile carpet of the shitty DIY recording studio against the scuffed white heels of his tennis shoes. The sweat in his eye he couldn't wipe away without missing a cue. Three old friends. One dead, two gone weird. Somehow, Miles had made it out. And he was the dumb one. They'd all known it. But here he was. He should call them. He knew he should call them. But every time he called them, he lost more and more of the teenagers he'd loved. The brothers he'd had at sixteen. They weren't any good, but they'd made music together. Without thinking ahead or planning it out. Together, they'd happened upon something they could never have had on their own—the urgent synchronicity of a messy, lurching song. You didn't get that with most people. Some never had it with anyone. He hadn't thought about them in years.

There was a time in his life when Miles thought marriage would be like a band. But his marriage was more like two people soloing over each other. Here, on a rural road outside of Baltimore, Miles listened to a record of what he and three friends had managed in a small room at a certain moment in time, and he finally saw it for what it was. Irreproducible. At least in the sense that the memory wouldn't exist to be reproduced by the company's hardware if Miles and his friends hadn't given four years of their afternoons and evenings to the endeavor in the first place. It was their life, and no one else's. It was horrible, but it wasn't half-bad. It was better than the memory, he decided, having the memory of the tape to listen to in the Egg. He didn't care that the tape wasn't real. It was still feeding Miles memories he'd forgotten, building ladders of association that would take him further back than he would ever have been able to go on his own.

They'd built a wonderful thing. Miles and the company had made a place you could go when the world was too much, or not enough, or when you needed to be reminded of exactly what it was, and why it was worth being a part of. Still, Miles was finding it hard to focus on the experience. His mind was wandering, and his thoughts were dipping away from the road and back again like barbed wire. There had to be some medical application for it. Something someone somewhere needed. He'd meant to do that at one point. When his father was sick, and illness was on his mind. Miles had more say with the company now, and the team members they'd imported from the lab would probably be thrilled at the opportunity. Lately, even those who'd chosen to stay were starting to grumble. He'd have made a note to look into it, but he had nothing to write with. He'd have thought about it more, but already he was looking away.

His wife was in the passenger seat trying on bras. He'd tried to get her exactly right, but the rendering would never be perfect. That was partly their fault, but it was also the nature of these things. No one remembered anything exactly as it was. Each time you remembered it, you lost details and your mind filled them in, traveling you further and further from the memory as it had been originally forged. He'd heard somewhere that the safest memories, the ones most reliably unaltered by those doing the remembering, were the memories stored in the mind of an amnesiac. Memories that couldn't be remembered. Still shaped by the limits of an individual's perception, those inaccessible memories, as he'd understood it, were the closest thing to accurate, as recall itself was actually an act of neurological reconstruction, with each new formation traveling the mind farther from a memory's original formation. It had been nothing but an abstract point to Miles until he was confronted with the simulated moles on his wife's neck.

They wouldn't stay put. And the shape of the divots in her back looked wrong too. She had a traveling pelvic scar that was perpetually self-correcting, drifting toward her belly button then snapping back into place above her hip. He tried to calm himself down. He tried to settle his mind, hoping that would crystallize his wife's itinerant features. But he was already distracted, already thinking of what she'd said earlier that night and wondering if, should he and his wife ever divorce, there would be a potential consent issue if the images of her conjured by the Egg too accurately captured her as she would be then, as his ex-wife, rather than simply replicating her as she had been when they were together, which felt like a body he should be allowed to remember.

"It gets rotten-smelling after a day," she said, showing him a beige bra without an underwire, explaining how it sometimes rolled into the folds under her breasts or bunched up. "Like expired half-and-half," she said.

He kept his eyes on the road, though he didn't need to. Still, it felt good to glance over every now and then, catching glimpses of her, rather than just sitting there, staring. He didn't want to leer.

She squinted, holding the underside of the bra up to his nose as if to prove it, but he didn't bother. Smell was still an issue. Getting the artificial odors they pumped in to associate believably with the different items encountered in a given experience had proved to be a massive undertaking, and one they were, for now, mostly failing at. There was a subjectivity to smell that, so far, had been impossible to replicate. For example, his wife had loved the smell of dirty diapers. She wasn't about to wear it as perfume, but she sometimes claimed to miss it. That smell, that time in their lives. Two young girls, and the constant presence of shit. For Miles, the smell had been a dirty palm pressed into his face. Objectively filthy. He was glad when it was over, when the whole house had resolved itself to shitting in private. How could you manufacture something like that? Horrible and heavenly. The same thing, but either way to either person, and, in that, the potential to change. There was an objectivity to replication that did not exist in lived experience, however dynamic, unpredictable, or detailed the replication could be made to feel.

The pumps were working on him. They felt surprisingly lifelike, though he had no idea what he was comparing them to, what exactly was supposed to be happening to him. Whatever it was, it felt real.

He worried his wife would hear them through the door, which made it hard to concentrate. His mind was wandering again, and he was struggling to hold the walls of the car together. To keep the scene along the side of the road from mutating into something more current. More local. His office. His house. Their neighborhood. His gate. Their life.

The company had put so much money and time and effort into making the pumps quiet, but however faint, you could still hear the undeniably crude sound of suction. Motors whirring. A low gurgling. Shameful, but good enough for their purposes. Nothing popular was perfect anyway. In fact, quality was becoming less and less relevant, as popularity established the context that allowed for quality—and therefore the potential for perfection— to develop. From the perspective of a company like his, by the time you were able to get something right, it was past time to move on.

Miles stopped. The woman going down on him was his wife and not his wife. The same hair color but pulled back. He wanted to shout but feared it would come out not in the experience, but in the house around him, drawing attention to where he was. What he was doing. Instead, he opened the car door and slid out from under her, onto the Baltimore asphalt.

Nothing hurt in the experiences, not unless you wanted it to. Even then, it was only a shadow. A pain flirtation. He looked back at the car, and there was his teenage daughter. A young woman in his wife's bra, grinning back at him from the passenger seat, her hair coming loose in its tie.

"Thank you," she said, reaching for the air where he'd been.

Miles jolted up and out of the Egg. He felt feral. Like the world was made of danger.

He hadn't built that. He hadn't wanted it. It was an awful joke. Someone else's awful joke. Or a glitch in the system. He'd been thinking about his children. His daughters. His wife. He hadn't been thinking at all. He left the room as quickly as he could. Even looking at the machine made him feel like he was going to jail.

✦

Miles took a long shower, not washing anything. He stood in the cold water, letting his heart settle. Maybe it hadn't been her. It was awful to think, but if it was some other child, not *his* child, that felt somehow better. Not what he'd wanted, but at least it wasn't. He couldn't bring himself to say it. He couldn't allow himself to even think it. He climbed out of the shower cold and wet, drip-drying onto the linen mat.

✦

Miles clipped his nails on the edge of the tub, drawing blood. Upstairs, his daughters were sleeping. Two rooms down, his wife was too. A smile on her face. Her red-stained teeth. Or maybe she only did that when she was pretending to sleep, when she knew he was watching. He'd never know for certain. Not without risking the loss of it to exposure.

Thank you.

He didn't want to think about it. He couldn't. Not

without needing to plunge his thumbs into his eyes. He lay in bed, pinching the skin around his wrist. Pulling it as tight as it would go.

He'd made an awful thing. An awful place where you could never be alone. Where other people could climb in, touch everything. Turn you against yourself. Turn what you loved into something reprehensible. You could turn it back, but what happened to you once you'd seen it? Once someone else had seen you see it? For a second, Miles thought he could smell the lamb. Or he remembered smelling the lamb. Years ago. From a grain of rice on his finger. It had to have been something in the wall. The thumps. The smell. He knew he wasn't smelling it, but there it was.

THIS WILL ALL BE OVER SOON

The thought of the latest threat kept coming to him, coiling through all his other thoughts like an eel. It wasn't what he wanted. It wasn't exactly what he wanted. But, after the evening he'd had, it was a thought that helped.

23

9:00 p.m.
Across the Street

Of all the threats so far, this was the only one that confused him. Like the others, it consisted of a typeset message delivered in an envelope bearing only his name, but the typeface was different, as well as the quality of the ink. It was elegant, but it wasn't nice. It smacked of effort and contained nothing but a location (Across the Street) and a time (steadily approaching). The others had asked him to think, whereas this one was only asking him to act.

Miles had no intention of going, but the boldness of the note intrigued him. Across the Street was a bar he knew, both the name and its location. At the time of night listed, the bar would be full of the after-dinner crowd, likely people he knew from work. Was that how this person wanted him to die, in front of the people most impressed with him? At least that's how he assumed his coworkers felt, those who didn't hate him. It didn't feel self-aggrandizing to say he'd accomplished something admirable with his time at the company. Even if they hated him, they couldn't deny all he'd done, or managed to get done.

The threat was further set apart from the others by the location of its delivery. Every other threat had been left at his home, dropped in through the door with the rest of the mail. But this one had arrived at work.

"Who sent this?" he asked the young woman making rounds with the mail.

She held her hand to her left ear, muting the noise-canceling earbud hidden within.

"Where'd it come from?" he said.

"Downstairs," she said.

"But from who?" he said.

"I just get the bags," she said.

Over the course of the day, mail and packages were brought to a room on the first floor where they were sorted and eventually picked up by the office manager or some unlucky delegate, then distributed around the office at five o'clock. It could take hours to get through it all, and Miles would have missed the note that day if he and Lily hadn't been working late again, preparing for a system-wide update meant to exponentially decrease the latency of their software—the distance between a thought and its experience. They were only supposed to have provided perfunctory approval, but instead they'd spent the last few hours hung up on an apparent rendering glitch, with little headway made after all that time and effort.

"It doesn't make sense," said Lily. "Everything works fine until the user, and whatever content they're generating, vanishes. Like Uriah fucking Heep. It's not a deletion, because the absence itself is there. It's like they're cloaked. Hidden within the program itself. Or by the program itself. It's like they're in there, but not thinking. Or they left without leaving. It's not possible. It shouldn't be happening. Am I boring you?"

Miles was staring at the threat, turning it in his hands. "Uriah Heep?" he said, trying to buy himself time.

"Focus," she said.

"Right," he said. "What do you make of this?"

He tried to hand her the note, but she leaned back, stretching her neck over her office chair, so her head dangled upside down. She used her left foot to set herself spinning.

"Okay," he said. "What do you want to do?"

"I really don't fucking care," she sang.

"Fine." Miles set the note aside. "Let's go in ourselves and, I don't know, delete the absences. Or fill them in with something else? Or make it like a contest somehow. Let the users handle it. Solve the puzzle, win a prize."

"The users are the ones creating the absences," she said. "Or they must be. It's like they're hiding from us in our own software."

"Then we remove every ill-behaved experience," he said, "and go from there."

"Can I be honest with you?" she said, still spinning.

"I thought you were being honest," he said.

"I'm so fucking bored by this," she continued. "It feels beyond my abilities as a creative to express. Probably because my skills as a creative have atrophied due to years of being assigned to shit like this. I was a fucking talent. I had promise. Now I have . . . a nothing problem? And you as my only companion. You know what I'd like to do?"

"Help me fix it?" he tried.

She was in an outward position on her loop, and she made a sound that came out like steam.

"I'd like to book a flight to Canada," she said, "and pay extra for the exit seat, so I can learn what it feels like to open one of those big fucking exit doors before I leap out of an airplane straddling the Sierras."

The blood pooling in her forehead was stark against the crease of her dyed-black hairline. Miles watched the vein over her left eye bulge like it could burst.

"I'm serious," she said. "I'm so fucking bored that I want to go to med school, become a doctor, and quit in the middle of my first appointment, just to give my father's ghost a second fucking heart attack."

"It's a mystery," said Miles. "How can that bore you? It's a challenge! A puzzle!"

It's not my problem, he was thinking, but he knew if Lily wasn't keeping an eye on it, no one would. And if no one was keeping an eye on it, it could someday, accidentally, be misinterpreted as his fault. Little black holes spelled out in trillions of lines of otherwise functional company code.

"We should have dealt with this before the update," he said.

Lily laughed.

"Seriously," he said. "Someone should have said something."

The absences had in fact been reported to them through official QA channels, then by IT, then by two people in customer service, and finally by the ignorable temp who'd taken it upon herself to look into the accumulating reports. But it wasn't until they were confronted by a team tasked with pushing a system-wide update that Miles and Lily had finally found themselves having to account for something they could not understand and were in no way prepared to handle.

Whatever the absences were, they seemed to be by design—though how and why remained to be seen—and ignoring them clearly wasn't doing any good. There were more and more each day. More and more nothing. User-generated absence.

"I need to go home," said Lily. "I can't think. My brain rejects nonsense. It won't abide it. I'm sorry."

"You could use a break," said Miles. "Look at this."

He handed Lily the note, and this time she took it.

"I've been getting death threats," he said. "This is the latest."

Lily took one look and crumpled the paper. She threw it into the waste basket with a tight arc. The wrong bin.

"Hey," he said.

"It's not a threat," she said. "It's a work thing. A mixer."

"No, it's not," said Miles. "That's not it."

"They've been planning it for weeks," she said.

Miles leaned over to retrieve the errant paper, propping himself with one palm on the carpet. He rose with what he'd hoped would be a smile, but he felt a drop of sweat in his eye turn the look sour.

"Hero of the people," she said.

"It's not that hard to do it right," he groaned, setting the paper in the adjacent bucket—the correct paper bin— before awkwardly wheeling back to Lily's side.

"It's not that hard," she said, "to focus on an irrelevant problem when faced with one that might actually be your responsibility."

"You think a death threat's irrelevant?"

"I was talking about your trash-can bullshit," she said. "You think you're the only one getting death threats?" She stopped spinning and stared at the screen for a second before typing something in, then spinning again.

Miles stewed. He hadn't meant to make this about the threats, but all he could think now was that Lily had no idea what she was talking about. No idea what he'd been going through, or how hard he'd worked to avoid making it her problem. Maybe she'd read some comments online, received a few emails, but he had a drawerful in his kitchen! He won.

"It's a fucking headache," she said, still spinning. "And not just the nothing problem—which, nice try, boss man—I mean, *allllll* of this." She drew out the length of the *l*'s as she dug her toes into the ergonomic carpet, completing one last rotation before halting her chair and staring back at Miles with a face full of blood.

"I've had a light bulb," she said, completing another arc. "A fucking epiphany."

"Yeah," he said, trying to sound provocatively annoyed. "What's that?"

"I quit," she said, "this shit."

"Right." He set his fingers over the keyboard without typing anything. "But can you at least pretend to care? People are cranking enough power to run several small villages into experiences that read back to us as . . . what, empty? They're empty? It doesn't make any sense. These users are still in there somewhere. Someone's done something. They've gone in and fiddled. There's an answer here."

"Fiddled, you fuck," she said, righting herself and tamping her hair back into place with her palms. "We have the same information, Miles. We're looking at the same screen. And what I'm seeing"—she pointed toward the code they'd been staring at for hours—"which I know you're seeing with me, are lines and lines of code rendering populated experiences that read back to us as empty. So, tell me, are you really asking me, *again*, if nothing is something?"

This is why people don't like to talk about death, thought Miles. The sudden presence of an absence as impossible to imagine as it is to account for. It spits in the face of whatever it is you're living your life thinking you know. Miles patted his pockets, searching for a pen. He wanted to write that down. He was sure he could use it somehow.

"If you're going to stare off and be so mutely unhelpful," said Lily, "could you at least close your mouth? You sound like a subway vent."

Miles folded his lips over his teeth and brought them together, hoping the sting of it would keep him focused on the task at hand.

"This is why people don't like to talk about death," he said.

"Fuck," said Lily. "Just tell me what you want to do. Tell me what you want to happen, and I'll do what I can over the next two weeks. We're so far up your rabbit's fucking asshole, I'm not about to claim I can solve this on my own, or that it can even be solved. But you're the genius, right? The visionary. Envision something. The rest of us will do our fucking best to make sense of it."

Miles tried to look sincere, which he could tell made his face look fat. But Lily was right. This was boring. Hours of conversation, and there was nothing new to say about their nothing problem. Nothing more to see. Only unfounded speculation, each explanation as implausible as the next, and Miles was starting to feel like he was opening an empty fridge for a third time, a fourth time, hoping, maybe somehow, maybe *this* time, there'd be food waiting.

He knew what he wanted to do; he just didn't know how to ask for it. He also knew she knew it already. In all likelihood, she'd figured it out a long time ago, which was why she was asking him outright to just say it. The problem was, he didn't know how to ask for what he wanted without making it sound like he didn't care, or like he didn't think it was a problem. Because he did care. Sort of. And it was a problem. At least it could be. It could someday become his problem, and if it someday became his problem, which was to say *a big problem*, it wouldn't be good at all for him to have been the one who'd dismissed the early warning signs. But if he were to reveal how he actually wanted to handle this, if he were to say outright what he truly wanted to do about their nothing problem, he would be admitting to Lily that she'd been right from the start: there was no reason for her to care, or no reason other than to try to save Miles's ass, which he knew from years of working with her was not of particular interest to Lily on its own.

"Okay," he said, carefully scanning her face for frustration. "If it's not a glitch. And we have no evidence of any breaches or any other security issues." He looked at the screen, where nothing had changed. He squinted, as if he might see something there that could turn an ambiguous nothing into a solvable problem. "I say we encrypt again." He took a dramatic pause while he wobbled his head, faking a moment of last-minute assessment, as if double-checking some obscure formula he'd been working on all this time. "Change the codes. Enter the next phase of testing with all new users. Then accept that we've offered them the freedom to alter these experiences however they like and leave it at that."

Miles tried not to smile or look hopeful. He tried to look like someone who was speaking plainly, describing the situation no more and no less than exactly as it was. The course of action being presented as not exactly desirable, but sensible given the circumstances.

"Maybe nothing's what they want," he said, "and that's all there is to it. So maybe we let them have their nothing and see what we can learn from studying that."

Lily smiled, giving Miles what he momentarily misread as permission to feel, for now, like he'd said the right thing.

"Spoken," she said. She stopped and knocked the last peanut butter pretzel into her palm from a white paper snack bag before popping it into her mouth. "Spoken," she started again, "like an asshole with too much something."

She powered down the monitor, peeling the optimism from Miles's face.

"You're leaving?" he said.

"I mean, if nothing's all we're doing," she said, "it can wait until morning." She rose from the office chair and spun it under an adjacent desk.

"Wait," he said. "Did you really mean what you said? Two weeks?"

He already knew the answer. At this point, asking Lily to repeat herself was the only tactic he had left of affording himself more time with her. In two weeks, she would be gone. His only work friend, though she honestly seemed to hate him. Even so, he liked her, and they'd worked together for years. He'd spent more hours of his life with Lily than with his own wife and children. That had to count for something.

"When this was just an idea," he said, "you stayed

because you knew you could pull it off. You knew if it was just me, I'd fuck it up, but with you here, we could do it. We did do it. I think we could do this too. But I know I can't do it on my own. I need you."

"And hell," she said, "is needy people. I stayed because I wanted time to figure out where I was headed. And sure, because I felt sorry for you. But now I'm bored, and boredom trumps sympathy, so I'm leaving. And fuck you."

Miles knew this was meant to hurt him, but it had the opposite effect. It moved him. No matter how much time you spent with a person, it was almost impossible to know how they honestly felt about you. Here, Lily was admitting that at least at one point in her life, she'd thought of him as someone worth caring for. She'd felt sorry for him. She'd acted on his behalf. She would never know how much that meant to him, because there was no way of admitting it to her without dissolving that precious sympathy into pity (which, knowing Lily, would leave her one degree shy of disgust).

"Okay," he said. "Now that you've thought about it, where will you go?" What he wanted to say was, *Take me with you.*

"You're not allowed to ask me that," she said.

"Really?" he said. This time he asked it because he honestly didn't know if it was true.

"Or it's rude or whatever," she said. She took a breath. "Miles, I want to tell you something, so you can never say no one told you, or you had no idea. Or that you didn't see it coming. You are creative, and you are talented . . ."

"Thank you," he said, coasting on the fumes of her sympathy admission.

"And if you do nothing but punt their problems for the rest of your life, you're going to see things slowly get worse, then rapidly get worse, until the damage is irreparable and you have no idea how you got into whatever horrible situation you're in, because no one, especially you, will have given any thought to what exactly it was that you were doing, or what the end result would be. In order to keep all this up," she said, "in order to continue as you have been for any length of time, you will have to keep forcing yourself to ignore everything beyond the scope of the specific problems you are facing at a given moment on their behalf. You will keep thinking the world is happening to you, and not the other way around. You will keep changing directions, and it will keep getting worse because you haven't considered the costs of your actions, only whether or not they lift the shit from your lap. You'll focus on what keeps you moving forward, until there's nowhere left to go. At which point, you'll have no idea where you are, who you are, or how to get back to where you came from."

Miles wondered if she'd practiced this speech. If she'd stood at home in front of a mirror thinking of him and of the day on which she would finally get the opportunity to encourage him to save his own life.

"But you do have a choice," she said. "You could get out now. You could find something you believe in doing because you believe it's worth having done. You could try to figure out what that is. Because this is a hole. And it's as deep as the time you buy for them. When you're done, you'll be at the bottom with your busted shovel, and they'll be gone. They'll be somewhere else with some new asshole solving new problems, making them more money. This isn't a job," she told him. "It's Charybdis."

"Can I say something?" he said.

"I'd rather you meditate on my speech," she said, "and put your response in a letter." She grabbed her things: a lanyard she refused to wear that got them in and out of the building and an air-gapped laptop she brought with her to and from work each morning.

"You can't leave," he said.

"Fuck off," she said, leaving.

"Would you wait?!"

When Lily turned, the anger on her face dissolved into an attempt to hold back laughter. Miles was only a few steps behind, crab-walking after her in his low-set office chair, desperate to keep up. He'd worried standing up would appear too theatrical, or worse, aggressive, so he'd committed himself to pursuit in a seated position, despite knowing that it would actively undermine the charm, authority, and sense of urgency he needed to land what it was he wanted to say.

He wanted to tell Lily he would miss her. He wanted to tell her he'd meant the things he'd been saying all this time, manipulations or not, and that without her, he would be worthless on his own. He also wanted to tell her it was hurting his opinion of her, that she was abandoning him the second she couldn't see a way forward without a clear strategy from leadership.

"I understand," he said, "that someone of your talent and intelligence would want to find a more proactive solution for our nothing problem. And what I'm saying is . . . Please help me. Help me do that. I can't just pack up and go find something to believe in. I'm sorry, but I can't. Maybe you can, but you don't know what it's like for me. You don't have kids. I can't just leave a job like this and start a bakery."

"I have a son," she said.

"I've done good in my life," Miles insisted, annoyed with the way she was looking at him, like he'd let her down once again by being so typically Miles. He would have known she had a son if she had told him. Or, if she *had* told him and he'd forgotten, wasn't forgetting important personal information about a coworker a human enough flaw to be forgiven this once? "I worked on a show," he said. "People loved it. They wrote papers."

Lily's efforts to hold back laughter finally failed her. She erupted. She waved her hands in front of her face like she was being plagued by birds.

"That's enough," she said. "That's enough. I can't take it. I'll see you."

"Why now?" he said. "Why take us so far just to walk away?"

Lily grew quiet. She took a moment to genuinely consider the question, as if she felt she couldn't leave the room until she'd found a final truth to tell him.

"I don't know," she said, at the end of all of that thinking. "I was good at it."

✦

Moments later, Miles sat alone in the office, staring at an indecipherable screen. He understood what it said, but not what it meant. He limply crabbed to the recycling again and fished out the erstwhile threat.

9:00 p.m.
Across the Street

Now. Across the Street.

If he was going to die, at least he could learn something. And something was better than nothing.

Miles put on his shoes, laced them up, and left the office.

24

The bar was thick with buttoned-up bodies, and Miles worried he was losing his mind. These people worked with him. They worked around him and above him. Each was a killer, but none was patient enough to have waited this long to do Miles in. That meant Lily was right. It was a work function. And the only pleasure he could find in the fact that she was leaving him for good was that he wouldn't have to admit this to her.

Miles was about to leave when a drink arrived. He'd ordered it, but only half-seriously. He sipped a sour whiskey through two straws and watched people disappear into a phone booth at the back of the room. Over the course of his drink ten people went in, and none came out. He pushed his way through the crowd, and as the phone booth closed around him, he discovered a door without a knob. He pushed it and nothing happened. He was alone with a black phone, the kind he should have known to expect. It was the only straightforward thing in the whole crooked place, but it still surprised him. He lifted the receiver and held its disembodied warmth to his ear. After a long, cool tone, he heard a voice.

"Yes," it said.

"Where's everyone going?" said Miles.

"I'm sorry?"

"I saw ten people come in here."

"Okay," said the voice, a little impatient.

"Wait," said Miles. "Is this a password thing?" He sipped his third whiskey sour. "You really want me to go outside and look it up on my phone? I mean, I already get it. Just let me in."

There was a sigh, and a click, before the line went dead. Miles pushed the door-shaped wall again, and this time it crept open. Inside the bar was another bar, dimly lit and full of promise. Red candles perched on invisible black barrels. He saw white shirts, gray teeth, and blank curiosity.

"I know you."

He'd been approached by a child, maybe twenty. It was stirring ice in an empty glass.

"Yeah?" said Miles. "Who am I?"

"We work together," said the child. "I'm Ted."

"Miles," said Miles.

"I know," said Ted. "Can I buy you a drink?"

An hour later, the room had narrowed to a barrel, a candle, and a cabinet's worth of empties.

"We should clear these," said Miles, rattling the glass.

"We should," said Ted, in a calm and supportive way.

"Were you always good with people?" said Miles. "Or did you learn it?"

Ted's talents, Miles had learned, were in talent management. He'd gone to school for it. He was hired by the company to oversee a small percentage of its high-profile users, which meant backdooring the company's interests by partnering with whichever users were creating the platform's most popular user-generated content.

"People are easy," said Ted, waving him off with infectious charm.

"You say that," said Miles, "because you're good at what you do."

Ted's job was to keep high-performing users engaged with the company's platform, to keep them inspired, to keep them from jumping to another company—but above all, to keep them creating content. The company needed a person like Ted because, while OEs were great, UGC was cheaper, faster, easier, and had fewer variables. Plus, it had the potential to be comparably successful, if edited and repackaged correctly. A single Ted could handle a hundred users at a time, and one user, they'd proved in the years since the platform had launched, had the potential to generate three to five times the profit of a single full-time designer. Not all of them. No more than a rare few, really. But it only took a small sample to set a standard the company could then use to make their next promise to shareholders, and to entice more and more users to optimistically generate more free content. Successful or not, each new user was valuable to the company from an

ARPDAU perspective, and, because content-generating users weren't employed by the company, the company had no professional loyalties or legal courtesies owed to them, regardless of how much their content came to benefit the company. It was all gravy. Pure frosting. The more users they had, the more UGC, and the more UGC, the more other users had to work with. It wasn't exactly win-win, but there was winning involved.

The company set it up so they had to do little more than wait and see which user-generated experiences attracted the most users. Then they sent in Ted to woo the user creating those experiences, keeping them excited about generating content for the company, for as long as the company was excited about keeping them generating that content. The Egg had the potential to change all of this, but so far neither Miles nor Ted had mentioned the Egg.

As Ted explained it, a little extra attention could almost double a user's output, and for certain users that meant an astronomical amount of playback. Ted's job was to make them feel special; and some of them, he said, were special. Others tended to burn out, or wane in popularity until they were eventually abandoned by the company, but that wasn't the company's problem. All the company did was provide a creative and professional outlet for those users who sought to distinguish themselves. It was up to the users to figure out some way of turning that work into a sustainable life. The company never outright asked these users to make anything, nor did their business model rely on them in any way. Or so was the line. As far as the company was concerned *harness* and *rely on* were worlds apart. In fact, there was something close to altruistic in what the company had been doing. They had created tools—tools the users could access at no personal cost. In addition to that, at least for certain users, the company provided small incentives and encouragements in the form of Ted.

"People aren't hard," said Ted.

"You mean that," said Miles. "I can tell by the way you keep repeating it."

Ted laughed. And when he laughed, he smiled, revealing that he had great teeth. Not perfect teeth. Just really good, crooked little teeth.

"I like your teeth," said Miles.

"Most people do," said Ted. "It's weird."

"Really?"

"It comes up a lot."

Miles looked at his watch, and it was all numbers. Time to go. He should have been leaving.

"What's it like?" said Ted.

"I can taste my hangover," said Miles. "It's in my throat already. Like, I can taste it. Right here." He rubbed the node of his Adam's apple.

"The Egg," said Ted.

"Oh, God," said Miles. "Just kill me."

"Hang on," said Ted. He was gone ten seconds, maybe twenty; then he was handing Miles something wrapped in crinkly paper.

"Is it a firecracker?" said Miles.

"Underberg," said Ted. "It's like medicine."

Miles took a closer look. He held it to his eye. It was a small brown bottle wrapped in caramel-colored paper.

"You crack it," said Ted. He twisted the paper off, along with a tiny hidden cap. "And suck it down." He put the bottle between two pursed lips and emptied it. "Gah," he said, tossing it to the floor.

Miles heard his sizzling breath. He thought he smelled smoke.

"Just like that," said Ted.

"Just like that," said Miles. He twisted the paper and twisted the paper. It wouldn't rip. He pinched a small fold of it between two fingers from each hand and worked out a tear. He tried again, and this time it came free.

"There you go," said Ted. "There you go!"

Miles tossed the paper into the ink of the room and unscrewed the green cap. He tilted his head back and held the bottle over his mouth. An acrid drop rattled his tongue, and he blinked, coughing. But nothing else came. To finish it, he had to shake the horrible thing like a ketchup bottle, drinking the rest of the poisonous liquid in gag-worthy spurts. It tasted awful. It felt wonderful. He asked for two more.

"I can feel my pupils dilating," Miles said.

"I can't believe you've never had it," said Ted.

"I don't really come to bars," said Miles.

"You should do it more," said Ted. "You're good at them."

An hour later, the barrel was clear. Ted was telling Miles about a dog he had that was very well-behaved.

"They have to know what to do all the time," he said. "You have to tell them. Otherwise, they get upset. They get nervous. People are almost always wrong about dogs. Dogs are like people. Most dogs are miserable. You have to tell them what they're supposed to do."

"I always wanted a dog," said Miles.

"You've never had a dog?" said Ted.

"I've never had a dog for as long as I would have liked," said Miles.

"It's so cool," said Ted.

"Dogs?" said Miles.

"That we're drinking together," said Ted. "That I'm drinking with you."

"I feel the same way," said Miles.

Ted shook his head.

"No," he said. "I came here because of you."

"I wasn't even going to come here tonight," said Miles. "I thought someone wanted to kill me."

"To the company, I mean. I'm from Virginia," said Ted.

"There you go," said Miles.

"You must hear that a lot," said Ted.

"It happens," said Miles, having never heard anything like it before in his life. He liked this kid. He was feeling better than he had in years.

"I mean, the Egg's probably going to put me out of a job," said Ted.

"No," said Miles. "No way. You're good with people. The Egg's got . . . problems. But being good with people is important. People are more important than eggs. And you're good with them. You're going to put *me* out of a job, Ted. You old honey-dripper. You snake-charmer."

"People aren't hard," said Ted. "The only thing to know is that it all goes somewhere. With people, everything matters. That's all there is to it."

"What are we doing?" said Miles. They were easing from foot to foot, halfway to stepping. At some point, Ted had started moving, and Miles had matched him. He hadn't given it any thought at first, but the strangeness of the scene was rapidly coiling itself around Miles's good time.

"We're dancing," said Ted.

There was no music. There was hardly any room for it.

"Can we drink more of those firecracker things?" said Miles.

"The Underbergs?" said Ted.

"The Underbergs!" said Miles.

They high-fived. Or shook hands. They touched, and Miles felt like crying. He told himself not to.

Ted was getting drinks, and Miles felt explosively good again. He felt light and concentrated, like he could manage a heist. Walk a tightrope. He was fine. There was no danger. He tore the brown paper and scrapped the cap.

"Sometimes," said Miles, "I hate this place."

"Sometimes I cry at Coke commercials," said Ted.

"I've done that," said Miles. "It feels good."

"Yeah," said Ted. He nodded. "It's good."

"But I don't hate this place," said Miles, realizing he actually kind of liked it here. He'd like to love it. "I really don't. I don't hate anything, honestly."

"That's good," said Ted. "That's a start."

"I feel really very happy here," said Miles. "I feel really very good."

25

Morning came like Drano—a bright cleansing of Miles's mess. He couldn't remember anything from his ride home. A car, maybe. A song that kept repeating in his head as sunlight stained the windows. If he'd slept at all the night before, his body didn't remember it.

It was all Miles could do to scrape himself out of bed, take a quick cold shower, pocket some ibuprofen, and push his hollow body back into the clothes he'd left on the floor, all so that he might arrive at the office a few minutes shy of ten o'clock, where he found an email summoning him to an urgent sync with a name he did not recognize, scheduled for the moment he'd sat down.

Seated across from an unknown manager, Miles was now struggling to keep his head up. He pinched his chin between his thumb and pointer finger, searching for opportunities to press his beleaguered eyelids together for more than half a second. None of it seemed to bother the unknown manager, who was smiling at Miles with genuine affection, though Miles had never seen this man before in his life.

"This isn't easy," said the manager. He was a boy, maybe twenty-six years old, with a shock of orange hair perched atop foam-blue roots. "But we hope you can understand our position."

It might have occurred to Miles to ask what exactly their position was, but he was distracted by the guns.

Two security guards flanked him, armed with real guns containing deadly bullets. Each of them had one strapped to his hip, hanging from a black belt cut from tactical fabric. Miles had imagined the average office security guard would carry something like a billy club, or a Taser, nothing more serious than that—but their company worked with private security for good reason. Their rules were their own.

"This is James," said the manager. "And this is Eli."

Miles was beginning to realize he had not been called here for some kind of congratulations.

"This is serious," said Miles, almost involuntarily, like a spasm. The hiccup made him self-conscious, and in a vain attempt to assert his mental acuity, he repeated himself. "Very serious."

"It's unfortunate," said the manager, rising, along with his desk, into a standing position. "But it's also simple." He put out his hand. "It's been an honor."

✦

James and Eli followed Miles out of the meeting room, through the open office. Miles wished he weren't so wobbly, though no one had looked up to watch him leave. They were working, or pretending to work; the result was the same. Collectively, they created the impression that they had no idea Miles was even there, let alone that he was leaving.

The company could have easily, if expensively, done the work of unbraiding the code to determine which of the two dozen beta testers had originated the horrors Miles experienced during his one night in the Egg, but it wouldn't change the fact that there was now a recording of him willingly engaging in oral sex with his teenage daughter inside one of the company's OEs. The company wasn't going to sort it out because they didn't need to know any more than they already did.

The severance was generous, and his swift exit, according to the company, would be the end of the issue. No crime had been committed, no other human being had been involved, or no human other than whoever it was who'd put the thought into Miles's experience. The consequences of that night were real, though the experience, he reminded himself, was not. Climbing into the elevator with James and Eli, Miles tried to soothe his burning shame by reminding himself that the company did not have the moral high ground here, regardless of what was on that video. His experience was far from the worst thing viewable on the company's platform. There were corners of it that could change you forever. But the company was cleaning house. On the off chance there was ever a leak, this was the way they would need to have handled the situation, so this was how they were handling it. Evil, in Miles's case, was a question of optics. But it wasn't all bad.

Miles didn't know what he was going to do, but he knew he didn't need to know. Not yet. He and his family would be fine. Now that the company was aware of the video, it would do everything in its power to keep it from surfacing. In some ways, his situation had improved. Miles knew he should feel relieved. It was absurd to feel shame over something that had nothing at all to do with you.

He told himself that as the security guards arranged themselves on either side of him in the elevator. One of them—either Eli or James, Miles had already forgotten—leaned on the handrail, jutting his hip so that the handle of his gun pointed out toward Miles. Miles couldn't help but stare. He wondered if Eli, or James, had ever drawn it. If he'd ever fired it out of necessity or fear. If he hadn't, Miles thought, did Eli, or James, live in fear of that day, or did he look forward to it?

"Is it loaded?" said Miles.

"What?" said Eli, or James. He righted himself, bringing his hips back into alignment.

"It's loaded," said James, or Eli, from the other side of Miles.

For twenty-four months, Miles would receive biweekly severance pay in the same amount as his paychecks. He would retain full benefits for that amount of time as well, though he was obligated to cancel his health insurance once he'd found a new job, which would be easy enough, given all he'd accomplished.

The abrupt departure would carry a stink, but, the company had assured him, he would have good references. They would hire him again themselves if they could. All in all, Miles had made out okay. He'd made out fine. He rode the elevator down, trying not to look at the guns.

A crew would arrive in the coming weeks to disassemble the Egg.

26

That night, Miles's younger daughter was inconsolable. Her first root canal was in the morning, and she was refusing to sleep, as if by doing so she could indefinitely delay the appointment.

Miles and his wife had taken turns trying to comfort her, but neither approach had done them any good. Miles had had three root canals himself, and his original plan of talking her through the procedure, demystifying it in that way, failed miserably. His daughter did not want the doctor to take away pieces of her tooth. She did not want the doctor to burrow into her gums and remove anything rotten.

"It's not rotten," she said, clutching the swollen pocket of her cheek.

"It's decay," said Miles. "That's why it hurts. Rot is decay, and decay is a part of life."

"Don't scare her," said his wife. "It's a bacterial infection. It won't hurt after they take it out."

"Take out the life?" said their daughter.

"Sweetie," said his wife. She tried to touch their

daughter's head, but the girl ducked away and buried her face in the pillow.

"Do you want to watch a video?" said Miles.

His daughter said no. She kicked and squirmed and trembled the bed. Miles and his wife seemed to be the only ones approaching midnight.

They'd spent their day apart, and in the few hours they'd been home, they'd barely said a word to each other about anything other than the root canal. Miles's wife had been with the new architect since early that morning, working on their ever-evolving home, while Miles had tried to eat up as many hours as he could by walking back to them from across town so that he could pretend he'd been at work. But when the city proved too bright for his arthritic skull, he'd eventually found a dank parklet where he could hide from the sun.

He sat there swallowing ibuprofen until his brain finally settled, dull but appeased. At four, he went into a bar and ordered an Underberg. He drank it like an idiot, sucking on the neck to keep it from spilling. It wasn't how he remembered it. It was horrible. But with two down, he did feel better. He could walk, at least. He burned through three miles of road before finally giving in and ordering a car. He collapsed into the back seat, where he immediately began to dream of spotted moths.

He was in a room full of spotted moths, and his wife was outside working at the door. He knew it would upset her to see them. He knew it would be alarming. He was trying to warn her without saying anything, because he knew that if he opened his mouth, the moths would swarm.

The driver woke him just outside his sturdy gate.

"This is yours?" said the driver, pointing.

"Yes," said Miles. "Yes, thank you." He patted the seat cushions. Looking for what, he didn't know.

"It's a weird place," said the driver, staring at the unexpected shape of Miles's home. "I like it."

"Thank you," said Miles.

"What do you call it?" said the driver.

"I have no idea," said Miles, releasing himself from the car.

He didn't know what he was going to say to his wife, or how much of today's story was even necessary to share. He didn't like to think about it, so he'd only done so in quick snatches over the course of the day—a thought here, a worry there. He told himself his explanation would come spontaneously to him in the moment, but as he approached his house all he felt was the gnawing panic of the ill-prepared. He felt like an actor in the wings, struggling to remember the first line of a play he had not bothered to read. He entered without a plan, pressing his lips together, mutely praying no one would ask him a direct question.

"We have a problem," his wife had said.

It hadn't pleased him to hear his daughter crying in the background, but he did catch himself feeling relief, hours later, when he and his wife were still occupied with the root-canal issue and rounding the corner on midnight.

He'd made it far enough without being forced to account for his day that he knew they would collapse into bed the moment they were free of this final task, and he would have at least one more morning to figure out his approach.

"I'll brush," said their daughter, talking into the pillow. "I'll brush all the time."

Unfortunately for them, it wasn't her failure to brush that had led to the infection that made the root canal necessary. Or not directly. A year ago, she'd had a cavity filled in her front tooth, an occasion for which she'd been unexpectedly excited.

"My sister has three," she'd said, and she'd happily gone in for the filling the following week. She'd even dealt surprisingly well with the pain, stealing glances for days at the white fin of porcelain now covering her canine. Her only complaint was that the filling wasn't silver like her sister's, though she'd eventually admitted that metal on a front tooth wasn't exactly what she wanted either.

Miles and his wife had counted themselves lucky then—it had all gone so well—but here they were only a few years later, and the damage done to their daughter's roots by the corner-cutting dentist they'd trusted with her filling had led to an infection, a painful abscess—swollen, pus-filled—in the pocket of her gums. Everything about the new situation was worse, including its solution. On top of that, her older sister had never had a root canal, and Miles and his wife had no idea how to convince her that this new procedure wouldn't end the same way the filling had ended—with more problems and more pain.

They'd tried all evening, before giving up, deciding to let their daughter sit up the whole night, if that's what she wanted. Maybe if she wore herself out, she would be easier to get into the chair in the morning. But if there was no easy way to do it, it would still get done. That much they understood.

Miles and his wife walked the long hall to their bedroom, trying not to react to the cries of their daughter. Miles hated his new home after dark. It felt as if the walls were in constant motion, designed to outsmart him. Rather than making the place feel airy and large, the profligate windows seemed to narrow each room into unpredictable shapes. Miles worried he'd run into a wall. He pinched the back of his wife's bathrobe, letting her lead him.

"I feel bad," he said, deciding at the last minute to leave the bedroom door open, as if being able to hear their daughter crying in the other room might somehow be a comfort.

"Yeah, well." His wife secured her bathrobe with a quick cinch and climbed into bed. "I think it's fair to say that wasn't your A game."

"I had a long day," he said.

"And a long night before that," she said.

"That was a work thing," he said. He felt his hangover stirring under six feet of ibuprofen.

"It's fine," she said. "But I don't feel sorry for you. I don't know why she's like this."

"Who?" he said.

"Your daughter," she said.

"I guess she's scared," he said.

"You guess," she said. She clicked out the light while Miles was still at the end of the bed, tugging at his socks.

"I can't see," he said.

"You need to see your socks to pull them off?" she said. Miles removed his socks in the dark and joined her on his side.

"You smell like a brewery," she said.

He sighed and rolled over, breathing in a new direction. He listened to his daughter whimper and moan in the other room. In a night, it would be over. She couldn't imagine the relief she'd feel. Miles was counting on that. That she'd be happier in the end.

"I can't get used to this house," he said.

"What about it?" said his wife.

"Any of it," he said. "It's like I can't see it."

"I think if you tried a little more to understand it," she said, "it'd be easier to feel comfortable in it."

"I tried," he said.

"I said a little more," she said. "I didn't say you didn't try. There's nothing else in the world quite like it. It's a unique conception, perfectly realized. Leo is a visionary. Sometimes, I think you don't understand what's right in front of you."

"That's what I'm saying," he said. "I don't."

"Mia's crying," said his older daughter.

They sat up, and her shadow was in the doorway, watching them. For how long, he couldn't know.

"It's a process," said his wife. "She's getting older. We

can't dash in there every time she cries, or she'll never learn to comfort herself."

"I can't sleep," said his daughter.

"It isn't about you," said his wife.

"Right," said his daughter, storming out.

"You're all on fire tonight," said his wife. She folded herself back into bed.

"You think she was listening to us?" said Miles, after a few seconds.

"Why would you say that?" said his wife.

"I worry sometimes that she sits outside the door," he said. "And listens."

"I don't want to hear what you worry," she said. "I want to sleep."

Even if he'd wanted to, it wasn't the right time to tell her about his job. His non-job. There was too much going on already, and his brain was only a quarter well. Plus, she was already on edge. All she wanted was to sleep. He could feel her waiting for him to make a misstep, and he didn't have the mental faculties he'd need to right himself again, so why bother. He'd been right from the start. This was the wiser choice. Tomorrow, maybe. In a few days. The timing had to be right, so he could tell her in a way that wouldn't amplify all the other problems that were rapidly closing in on them. There had to be a way of doing it without hurting them, or not as much. He would figure it out. He just needed time. Everything would be fine.

"He's moving in," said his wife.

"Who?" said Miles.

"I was going to tell you in the morning, but the night's already fucked," she said.

"I'm sorry," said Miles, "but I have no idea what you're talking about."

"It's his anyway," said his wife. "You know this. So can you make one thing easy?"

Miles pushed his chin to his chest. It would feel better to belch, but he was already distracted enough with hating himself. He didn't want to make it worse. He tried to focus and piece his wife's meaning together on his own, while she grew silent and listened to him do just that. She had to be talking about the architect. He'd brought up the idea before, though never officially. Something about the distance between him and the house needing to close before he could fully separate himself from it. And she was right. Technically, the basement belonged to him. At least for now. Miles's wife was telling him that, at some point along the way, a decision had been made. Though what she was describing was completely out of hand, bordering on unreal, she'd said it with enough casual seriousness that Miles couldn't help feeling that he should have somehow seen this coming.

Over the past year, Miles had grown accustomed to saying yes without thinking, approving whatever the redesign called for without opening himself to potential irritation by too closely considering the reality of some of the requests being brought to him by his wife on the architect's behalf. The ideas were making less and less sense to him, so Miles had decided to set them aside, pushing them out of the foreground of conscious thought, if only to survive through the more immediate problems of each day.

The architect had been his wife's project from the start. She'd drawn him in. Thrown the right parties. Invested in the right artists. Overall, she'd spent ten months establishing a relationship with the architect, before pitching him the idea of redesigning their home the day after the architect's third wife had left him, when she knew he would be desperate to throw himself into his work. The consequent redesign had taken several years, the first six months of which were billed as "ideological gestation," but as the project grew and became more complicated, Miles had started to suspect his wife was drawn more to the idea of the home the architect was drawing up for them than to the enigmatic features in which the architect had actually encased them.

With no way to prove his theory and no interest in the aftermath of presenting such a roundly unsupported claim, Miles had gone ahead and invested incalculable sums into the redesign (in reality, they were not incalculable but had been calculated and presented to Miles several times for his approval), because the only thing that had really mattered to him at the time was that the whole confounding project of it all was making his wife happy. She claimed to be completely in love with whatever it was that was happening to their home. It was all she ever wanted to talk about, all she seemed to be thinking about when they were talking about anything else. It might have bothered

Miles, how preoccupied she'd become, if she hadn't been so infectiously drunk with anticipatory delight, which was something Miles hadn't experienced since, well, since they were falling in love.

Happy to see her happy, content to feed off his wife's accumulating joy, Miles had agreed—he couldn't believe it now, how stupid he'd been—he had *agreed* to grant the architect a temporary easement on the soil one hundred feet below their house, where the architect was going to build a basement, a bunker, a subterranean dwelling that would serve as a shelter for Miles and his family in case of emergency. It would have a private entrance, its own plumbing, separate security, the works. Why the architect had wanted the easement made as much sense to Miles as anything else the architect had requested. He'd claimed to want total freedom with the finishing touches, or that's what Miles's wife had relayed to him. She'd said the architect needed out from under the yoke of their permission, relief from the pressure of carrying their presence with him mentally wherever he went. He wanted the last note played to be his, and he wanted to perform it without a single thought for anyone else in the world.

"We won't know he's there," she said.

"No," said Miles. "No, I don't think so. It's too creepy."

"It's his baby," said his wife. "And he's about to hand it over to you. Imagine if our daughters were being moved somewhere, their care handed over to the highest bidder, and your only opportunity to be near them, to see what became of them, was to live below them. You'd take it."

"What?" he said.

"You have to think of the house as his child, Miles. This is how he's saying goodbye. It sounds silly to you, but from that perspective, it could be argued that he's being quite reasonable."

"Who would argue that?" said Miles. "It's not his child. It's our house."

"I wish you'd done the reading," she said. "If you'd bothered with it, I really think you'd understand. It's all temporary."

"You could explain it," said Miles.

"I can't just explain it," she said. "And why's that my responsibility? You have to arrive at some of these ideas on your own, in your own time. You should have done it. I know you could have."

"Sh," said Miles. He sat up, alert.

"What?" she said.

"I thought I heard someone," he said. "Outside the door."

"Miles," she said, "let it go. No one wants to hurt you."

"And what if he can hear us down there?" he said. "What if he listens? What if he learns I didn't do the reading, and decides not to gives us his child?"

"No one cares about what you didn't do," she said. "We all have too many things to account for."

For a fleeting moment, Miles felt compelled to tell her everything that had happened to him that morning, to pore over all the firsthand evidence he'd recently collected to the contrary of her point. Because, accounting-wise, what he hadn't done had become quite significant to the both of them. But instead of saying anything, he focused on his pillow. He thought about the feeling of the material that cradled his head, and how comfortable it was. He told himself to feel grateful for that feeling. He knew he should. He told himself that it could be enough. If he could do it, that is. Feel grateful.

"Miles," she said.

"No one cares?" he said.

"You know what I mean. No one but us. Your wife and daughters."

And Ted, thought Miles. There was also Ted. Ted cared. Miles wished it was the night before. He wished there was a way to escape back to that feeling, and he had the strong, sudden urge to run toward the darkness with Ted. He felt weak. He had nothing in him but the will to evaporate, and here was his wife, keeping him up. Of all the nights this could be happening, why tonight? One daughter was crying, while the other sat in the hall seething, and his wife wanted a man to move into their basement. He wished he knew how to handle this all very well. He wished he had an effortless touch with things, and a caring and attentive presence. He didn't want to ignore them, but he needed a moment. He needed all of it to stop for one moment, so he could remember how he'd wound up here in the first place, what he was doing and why. He wanted to start again so that this time he might handle it all perfectly. He believed he had the potential for that. He believed the odds were reasonably good that he could get it right.

"What would you do," he said, "if my stalker was in the house? Right now."

"Miles," she said.

"I'm serious," he said. "What would you do?"

His wife sighed. He heard the will to fight leave her body like steam.

"And what?" she said. "He's in the house, and what?"

"I don't know," he said. "He strangles me with a wire?"

He heard her eyelids shift wetly.

"I don't know," she said. "I guess I'd grieve."

He hadn't been expecting that. He was stirred finally into a grateful feeling, and the pain in his temple lifted.

"That's nice," said Miles. He searched for something else to say. Something that would let her know how much this meant to him.

"He asked me to go with him," she said, after a moment.

"Who?" said Miles, still thinking through how exactly he wanted to explain what he was experiencing.

"Leo," she said.

"Leo?" he said.

"Into the basement," she said.

Miles pulled himself into a seated position.

"You're doing what?" he said.

"I didn't say I was doing it," she said. "But if I did, it would only be until he's finished."

"If you're not going," he said, "then why are you bringing it up?"

"Because I'm thinking about it," she said.

"About what?" he said.

"About going."

"So you're leaving," he said.

"I'm not leaving," she said. "Even if I went, I'd be staying and living with Leo." She tugged the comforter from his lap, coiling it between her legs. "You're not going to say anything?" she said.

Miles knew better than to react from a place of pure emotion. The day had been too difficult, too long, and he was having more thoughts and feelings than he would be able to successfully express right now without making things very, very bad. So Miles waited, and his wife grew silent, and he spun the wheel at the back of his mind, blankly offering up the first alternative to hurt and anger and jealousy and rage that presented itself.

"Okay," he said.

He sank into the bed again, and his wife released the comforter so that he could pull it back over his shoulders with her warmth still in it.

"Okay," she said. "Thank you."

part four

thank you

27

Weeks went by, and the plan did not change. The root canal came and went. The pain was gone—it stayed gone—but his younger daughter grew sullen and withdrawn. She asked for binoculars, a book on the wild birds of Northern California. He spoiled her and her sister whenever he could, dodging questions about their mother. She wasn't leaving, he told them. This wasn't forever. He said those things without feeling them, hoping to make them true.

✦

The month after his wife left, Miles installed a pool in the middle of what felt like the living room but was actually part of the backyard. This was against explicit instruction left by the architect via his wife, but the backyard was aboveground: Miles's domain. And the pool was one of his favorite decisions.

Swimming was doing his older daughter good. She'd committed herself to it, and he wanted to encourage it. Miles had never been a good swimmer himself, but he'd watched a few training videos online, and after observing what he perceived to be his daughter's athletic plateau, he'd emailed a few times with a woman who'd written a book on swimming technique for racers. His daughter was powerful, but not fast, he explained. Her strokes were awkward and inefficient, relying almost entirely on strength for speed. The author had given him some pointers before politely severing contact.

Miles tried not to take it personally. He reminded himself that he had no real way of knowing just how complicated another person's life could be, especially one he'd never met. She was busy. Her hands were tied. There were countless things that could have been keeping her from the keyboard. But still, it couldn't have been all that hard to dash off a quick email to that effect.

Miles focused on moving on. He told his daughters he was going to work, and he walked the city—the same route each day—looking for metaphors in the trunk of a tree that had swallowed a road sign, or the fact that the billboards seemed to change daily, each for a new product that felt more incomprehensible to him than the last, or in the distinct variations he noticed in the same bleached-out laminate decal that hung in the window of every laundromat in the city: a blond businesswoman smiling out from behind a sewing machine, her face, or her hands, or her teeth uniquely cracked and faded from the sun. The best he could come up with was a vague sense of association, like he wasn't the only one losing detail, wearing down, or on the verge of being consumed. It was a stretch and a bleak feeling made worse by the fact that Miles knew there was nothing to be gained from surrendering himself to it. He could not wallow in the deterioration of a city. He needed to take some kind of action in his own immediate life, but it had to be the right kind of action. He'd taken too many left turns lately. He knew he had to come up with a fitting response to the demands of each day, but in the absence of a clear path forward, he settled on a temporary resolution to not linger.

He bought a stack of books with the word *You* in the title. He read the introductions to most of them, taking excessively thorough notes that sometimes outran the number of pages comprising the introduction itself. He set the goal of living moment to moment, telling himself to avoid obsessing over what had happened before in favor of focusing on what was directly in front of him.

All this time, Miles saw nothing of the architect. He'd hoped for as much, but found that in the man's absence he was starting to feel like the architect was somehow everywhere, listening through the floor, watching from the recesses of every walk-in closet, living in the walls of Miles's incomprehensible home.

In general, life was beginning to feel so cruel and unpredictable that when Miles came home one day and found the last threat waiting for him in the hallway, just below the mail slot, he was only a little surprised to find that it provided him a feeling of relief. One of the few reliable constants in his life, the threats had also, somewhere along the way, started to appear to Miles as inextricably linked to his good fortune. They were part of a larger cosmic design meant to balance out the good in his life with benign reminders of his own mortality. He'd even started to think that the threats could be included in his public archive, studied long after his death (of peaceful, natural causes), and that maybe one day some hypermotivated true crime author would use the well-preserved, well-cataloged threats to track down and confront the person responsible. Or the person responsible would come forward on their own and volunteer to sit down for a prolonged interview about what had inspired the notes in the first place, as well as what had kept them from following through with their plan—Miles's advances in the field of virtual reality experiences, maybe. He didn't think it was arrogant to acknowledge the scope and success of his idea, however disgracefully his career had ended. If anything, Miles felt he made too little of his accomplishments. He'd shown the world where it needed to go and helped build the teams who'd executed on that vision. He'd contributed genuine moments of happiness to the lives of countless people. How could you want to kill a person like that? How could you continue to want them dead?

Miles carried the threat into the kitchen and placed the opened envelope on the table.

"Girls," he called.

In the distance, he heard a glass door whoosh shut, and he was alone again with the threat. Everything else in his life had changed, except for these. Whoever was sending the threats still cared enough to check in on him, to let him know they were still thinking of him, after all this time. It was almost sweet.

THANK YOU

The last threat didn't read like a threat at all, but when Miles finally saw the ink-black words floating in eggshell white, years of hard-won indifference fell away.

While each of the other threats had felt like a promise, a possibility, an idea for the future if not a glimpse of the future itself, this one seemed to point backward, as if some final, awful thing had already happened to Miles and he had somehow managed to miss it.

Miles stood in the kitchen, reading and rereading the threat until its edges began to blur and his focus shifted to the backs of his hands. They were mottled pink and yellow, covered with sunspots. They looked larger than they had in the past, as if the rest of him had been shrinking. They were his father's hands. His eyes were getting tired. He was starting to see things. And his ankles were sore. Lately, he had to be careful to stand up the right way, or risk a shooting pain up the back of his leg. His thighs had already given out on one of his walks, bringing him to his knees outside his office. His old office. To get up, he'd had to palm the city pavement, which had a sickening mealy firmness to it that stayed with him the rest of the week, making it psychologically difficult to eat sandwiches or other finger foods. He no longer had the strength or the skill to fight off another human. He wouldn't be able to run for very long, or very fast, if someone came for him.

Miles made up his mind to shred the last threat, burying it deep in the paperwork of the recycling can. It belonged with the others, boxed up in a closet Miles had been slowly, clumsily taking over since his wife moved out. But Miles couldn't bring himself to add it. He didn't want to think about. He didn't like the way the threat was making him feel. It was making him feel old.

Miles washed his hands and dried them. He held his fingertips to his nose, searching for the smell of the threat, but found only the oily and acidic combination of cedar and lye. He turned away with a new thought in mind— he could find his younger daughter and ask her about the birdbaths she'd been installing, or he could email the author again and ask her if he'd done something to offend her, if there was some reason she was ignoring him so completely—but he was greeted by the last threat's opened envelope, still waiting on the kitchen table behind him. Though he'd set it down just moments ago, he had already forgotten about it.

MILES

One word, in the same elegant type as the threat. No postmark. No return address. It stared back at him from the middle of the room, victorious.

If the last threat worried him, the presence of the envelope on the table took things one step further. Miles was afraid again. He was seized—as he had been on the first day, the second note in his hand—by a hopeless and paralyzing recognition of the inevitability of his own death.

After the years he'd spent learning to live with the threats, trying to get on with his life, it took nothing more than a slip of paper in a cream-colored envelope and a single handwritten word to undo it all. It didn't seem fair. He felt lied to. More than anything, the sudden return of that initial fear made him feel incapable of going through the process of shedding it all over again. He was too tired. Too old. He'd been done with it for years. But, like flies from the freezer reintroduced to the warmth of the sun, the old fear had shaken off its stillness and taken flight at the simple sight of pen on paper.

In the minutes that followed, nothing that occurred to Miles was useful, or peaceful, or productive. He was overwhelmed, standing at the kitchen table, turning old thoughts like diamonds, reexamining each like evidence from a crime scene, until he finally came to an idea that held him.

Miles had once been proud of his ability to resist the desire to obsess over the absence of postmarks or return addresses on the envelopes. He'd focused instead on moving on with his life, getting back to normal. He'd been happy to deny himself the mental image of a person approaching the mail slot, before or after the day's delivery, sliding the notes through, then turning to walk up the street on which he, his wife, and their two daughters lived. He'd been happy to avoid those thoughts because they did nothing but add yet another uncomfortable wrinkle to Miles's overwhelmingly impotent feeling at having nothing to do but wait for a hostile party to make their move before he could respond. And for a while, it had worked. With time, and more notes, the effect Miles had hoped for was finally, eventually, achieved. The notes had lost their potency, but they were always there, always mixed in with the daily mail by the front door, waiting to assert themselves. For years, that had not changed. What had changed, however, was his home.

Staring at the last envelope there on the kitchen table, Miles no longer felt indifferent to the absence of postmarks. Among myriad other inexplicable decisions, the house's new design had moved the front door several hundred feet back from the street, and the entrance to the long, winding path that would lead someone to their mail slot was now, and had been for some time, guarded by a spectacularly wooden gate. You'd need a battering ram to get through it. Or you'd need to be inside already.

Miles briefly entertained the idea of a sinister mail carrier, but theirs had changed so many times over the years that it was hard for him to imagine himself at the center of a U.S. Postal Service–wide conspiracy. And security would have notified him of any barbed-wire-shredded strangers slinking over the perimeter's fences. He wanted to blame the architect, but that wouldn't be so different from blaming the mail carrier. There weren't many people who'd been in his life long enough, and who were still close enough to him now, to realistically pull something like this off. Miles didn't know what to think. He didn't want to be thinking what he was.

Had the note read something different—something more in keeping with the generally existential vibe the threats had settled into over time—his fear might have passed more quickly. He might have folded the laundry. Ridden a bicycle. Moved money between investment accounts. Applied for jobs. But the wording of the threat, combined with the absence of a postmark, sent Miles circling back to a long-abandoned theory he'd once been able to bring himself to laugh at, but could now only consider with the gravity of a man who has somehow managed to miss his own death.

THANK YOU

The two words his daughter had said to him in the Egg. Or a vision of his daughter. He didn't want to think about it. But still. *Thank you.* He could hear the words in her voice. He could picture the work of her mouth, shaping them. It wasn't real, and it was hardly evidence, but it was there.

28

Miles had a drink. He started drinking. He accepted that it was a process, finding your way back to not thinking about something. It was a process, and he was starting it.

He and his wife had almost sent their daughter away. Aside from the incidents with her younger sister, his daughter had been unhappy for so long that there was surely risk of some permanent subterranean effect. They'd never told her how close they'd come to shipping her off, but maybe they'd acted differently around her once they'd had the idea. Maybe she'd overheard them talking about it or felt it in the air. Miles didn't know. In all likelihood, he never would.

If she wasn't angry before, the looming threat of exile could have been enough to turn her. If they'd scared her, maybe she'd wanted to do the same to them. She had always been subtly vindictive. Quietly spiteful. Obviously smart. If there was ever a score to settle, Miles knew his daughter could reliably deliver.

When she was much younger, Miles had forgotten to bring home the ice cream she liked from the grocery store, and he'd refused to go back out or place an order just for them. She'd been quiet the rest of the evening, but after the house had gone to bed, she'd stayed up late calling ancient, scammy psychic hotlines, leaving the calls running until she'd racked up a phone bill of close to eight thousand dollars.

He confronted her with the bill when it came.

"Did you place these calls?" he said, reading from the list: California Psychics, Northern California Psychics, Southern California Psychics—all resoundingly unclever names, especially for individuals purporting to have supernatural abilities.

"Yes," said his daughter, interrupting the list. She continued with eerie calm, holding eye contact Miles couldn't bring himself to break. "This is the kind of thing that happens," she said, "when we can't rely on one another."

✦

Miles went out back, where his daughter was swimming.

If she was still angry, she wasn't taking it out on her sister anymore. Her attitude was generally negative, but it came out in subtle ways. Everything was an imposition. She sighed and groaned. She slammed doors. Miles wasn't sure why she'd taken to swimming—he only knew she did it a lot—but he assumed her interest in it, at least part of it, came from the fact that when she was swimming the rest of the world was held at a distance.

"Maya," he said.

She ignored him or didn't hear him. She kept swimming.

Miles appreciated his daughter's determination. She was training more than ever, and he had noticed some improvements, perhaps because of his notes. In any case, she was placing in meets at school, and practicing longer hours, with more difficult drills.

"Maya," he said, a little louder this time.

She reached the end of the pool and turned back, pushing off. Again and again, the same movement. It was obvious she liked to wear herself out. At least that seemed to be her goal when she was swimming at home. She was always pushing herself, trying for more. He wondered if that's why she wasn't placing more often. Improper training. A psychological barrier. A lack of finesse, or athletic intelligence. She was smart, but maybe her heart wasn't in it. Or maybe she was smart in the wrong way. Maybe her mind was split, her focus elsewhere. Like the second half of that trip to Texas, when she'd been working so hard to stay busy. It was a long time ago, and she had changed . . . But how much?

Miles appreciated his daughter's determination, but he sometimes found it hard to believe that this was all that was left of her. This wet and worn-out person. When she was younger, she'd been curious. Inventive. Those were among the many attributes that seemed to be drying up with age. More and more, she was drawn to routine. She was waking up at the same time every morning, swimming two or three sessions a day, eating weighed-out and intentionally proportioned meals. Schedule, repetition, order, habit—things Miles had never found useful and therefore found suspicious.

"Can we talk?" he said, watching her turn again and swim away.

There were dinners like this. Miles would attempt some conversational inroad, or ask his daughter a plain, benign question, and she would so convincingly act as if she hadn't heard him that he would let it go, assuming she was preoccupied with something internal and urgent. Occasionally, Miles caught himself thinking of her as a stranger, as some soft-spoken criminal who'd kidnapped his child and was keeping her from him without even the courtesy of a ransom, but the truth was far less exciting than all of that. The truth was that his daughter was changing faster than he could incorporate into his methods of approach. And even if they had been talking more, he knew she likely wouldn't be able to explain what she was going through. He could remember the loneliness of that age, feeling overwhelmed by the accumulating changes in one's life, like the moment he finally understood some alienating new part of himself, the knowledge seemed to be somehow no longer useful. Life moved on. If he hoped to have any chance of keeping up, Miles had to move on as well.

"Maya," he said, giving up. Giving in to the idea that this was all that was left of them, of Miles and his daughter. This was the best they could do.

Despite the popularity of the adage, Miles did not believe youth was wasted on the young. The pleasures of youth were the by-product of its shallowness, the ability to feel things deeply and then forget them, to hurry from one moment to the next, taking life as for granted as possible. It wasn't a waste; it was the point.

When he was young, Miles had been able to comfortably shed what he knew he did not need. He could change, adapt, reset, confident that each new version of himself was somehow his most authentic self. But as he'd grown older, Miles's life had started to accumulate. The more it did, the more he clung, by nostalgic choice or irrepressible pathology, to those bits of past selves he could not shed, carrying them around with him wherever he went like power cables for equipment he no longer owned. He was losing his ability to sort the important from the insignificant, to distinguish between who he had been, who he thought he should be, and who he truly was.

Miles sat at the edge of the pool, wondering if he could ask his daughter outright about the threats. He tried to imagine a desirable outcome. He tried to calculate risk versus reward, to understand what he wanted from the conversation, and what he would say if she willingly confessed. It would be the first time he'd had a conversation of this level of importance on his own, without his wife there to back him up or contradict him. He didn't know if that excited or terrified him. He decided that it would be better to let his daughter tire herself out before trying too hard to get her attention. A conversation like this could easily become confrontational, and he didn't want to push it. But he did want to know.

Miles left his daughter in the pool and wandered the dizzying chambers of his empty home, reviewing the strategies available to him for mitigating unnecessary harm or distress. He would wait for her in her room, on the corner of the bed, where their eyes would be level. Her floor would be lined with water cups, as it always was. Some fresh. Others collecting dust. He would hunch his shoulders to reduce his size, lower his chin, and add a deferential tilt to his imposingly large head. He would not ask her outright about the notes. Instead, he would set her up for the admission, cultivate a safe space, and let her walk into the trap. Then they could talk.

Miles searched for the door to her bedroom, and the longer it took, the more convinced he became that this had been the plan all along. His wife would join the architect in the basement, but only after the house had been rendered unnavigable to her fool of a husband, a final collaborative act of retribution for a crime Miles wasn't aware of having committed. Perhaps they hoped it would drive him mad like an Italian duke inheriting the now-haunted castle of a brother he'd murdered to secure the bequest. Afterward, they could triumphantly reemerge, like those who've spent nuclear winter hiding in a subterranean bunker, and, blinking out over the carnage of the world, they could begin again.

By the time Miles found the door he'd been looking for, he was feeling better. Not much, but enough to proceed. After all, if it was true, it wasn't all bad. If it was her, and the death threats he'd been receiving all this time were in fact nothing more than his older daughter's desperate attempt to make contact with him, it would be the most consistent and intimate form of communication they'd shared since she was a little girl. If the notes were hers, it was almost like they'd grown so far apart from each other that they'd looped back around again, vibrating together in the abstract proximity of intense feeling. Her anger, his fear. It was a lonely kind of closeness, but it was better than the alternative.

Opening the door, Miles discovered the water cups he'd imagined lining the floor by her bed. When he saw them, his lonely and unproductive thoughts evaporated. He felt a call to feel moved. He knew his daughter better than he sometimes feared. She was not a total stranger. Not yet anyway. She was a person he'd spent time with, and, maybe, he caught himself beginning to hope, it wasn't too late for them.

Miles arranged himself on the edge of her bed exactly as he'd pictured. He tilted his head deferentially.

✦

When his daughter finally arrived, she was carrying her wet clothes in a linen bag drooped over her shoulder. She stopped herself in the doorway and studied her father.

"What's wrong with your neck?" she said, watching him curiously as he struggled with where to begin.

"Honey," he said, the first and last time he ever called her that, "how are you?"

"What?" she said, before correcting herself. "I mean, what do you mean?"

He reminded himself not to push.

"I'm just here," he said. "To talk. To say hi, I mean. Hello."

"Hi," she said.

"Actually," he said, "I want to talk to you about something."

"Right," she said.

"But I'm not sure how to ask it," he said.

"You can just ask," she said.

"I guess that'd be simplest."

"Can I hang up my stuff first?" She eyed him as she moved casually into the room.

Miles could tell he hadn't yet made the conversational inroads necessary for them to have the talk he hoped to soon be having, and he felt the need to accomplish at least that much before losing her to a task.

His daughters understood their new groundbreaking punishment of a home better than he ever could or would ever care to. If she left the room, it was possible he'd never find her again. He tried to put the mystifying network of hallways in which he now lived out of his mind. He tried to calm himself. He tried not to wonder if his wife and the architect were listening to all of this from below. If the vibrations in the earth had subconsciously alerted them to an awkward conversation playing out overhead.

"Sure," he said. "But before you do . . . just one thing."

He searched for the right way to say it. "You know I know I could never know you. Right?"

"What?" she said, before correcting herself. "I mean, what do you mean?"

"I mean," he tried again, "I couldn't know what it's like."

"What what's like?" she said.

"What I said," he said. "To be you."

"Right," she said. "Yeah, I know that. That's like the whole thing right now."

"Right," he said. "Good." Miles was trying to sound calm. If he wasn't careful, the conversation would be over before it began. "But, I mean . . . However old you are, it's always going to be the case," he said. "Or that's what I've been thinking. Right?"

"However old I am?" she said.

"What I mean," he said, "is it will always be the case, regardless of your age. What I'm saying, that is."

"How old am I?" she said, studying his face for any hesitation.

Miles hesitated. He knew the answer. He did. But the way she'd said it sent all the thoughts fleeing from his mind, and he now sat emptily before her, with only the most basic elements of himself slowly coming back into focus. Miles. Home. Daughter. Something. She was no longer ten; he knew that much. Time had passed, but how much of it?

"Dad!" she said.

"It's confusing," he said. "To hear you ask it. That's all. But I know the answer. I was there. So now it's my turn."

"This is why you're all embarrassed-looking?" she said. "This is what you wanted to say?"

"I look embarrassing?" he said.

"No," she said. She lowered her bag from her shoulder. "You look *embarrassed*. You *are* embarrassing."

"Come on," he said.

"I mean, objectively," she said.

"That's not how words like *embarrassing* work," he said. "You literally can't be objectively embarrassing. It's a subjective response."

"Is *this* what you wanted to talk about?" she said.

"No," he said. "Or I don't know. Sort of. You believe me, right? I know how old you are."

"I need to hang my stuff," she said. "It's dripping." Her gaze followed the falling water to where it was gathering at her feet.

"It's stone," said Miles, gesturing at the cold, gray floor, hoping he had described it accurately.

"Mom said it's terrazzo," she said, still staring at the floor, where each new drop grew the edges of a small, accumulating puddle into unpredictable shapes.

Miles watched the water, too, trying to do math in his head, but he could feel himself getting irritated, which he knew was an unhelpful response that would move him further from his goal of making his daughter comfortable enough to talk to him about something she might have been hiding for years.

"Can I try again?" he said.

"Okay," she said.

"I think my problem," he said, after several seconds, "is that I don't know where to start."

"That's not your problem," she said.

"It isn't?" he said.

"No," she said. "You already started."

"Right," he said.

Miles took a loaded breath, trying to gather his thoughts.

He was making a mess of this. So far, everything he'd said had landed askew, missed the mark, scorched lakes and forests instead of bunkers and silos. It was his fault if it was her. Faced with a challenging child, Miles and his wife had done little more than fret and argue before deciding to send her away. They'd done nothing to help her. Nothing to let her know it was okay, that they loved her regardless. It made sense to him if she was angry about that. It made sense that she'd be desperate for some way to tell him.

Still, Miles felt an unanticipated rush of relief at the thought of a resolution so close to home. And in the space provided by that relief, he felt an almost unbearable, crushing love for his daughter. Her bold presence. Her unfettered severity. It was a heartbreaking but satisfying idea that a lifetime of threats could be nothing more than the product of an eternally angry and strangely intelligent young woman looking to rattle her fragile father. If it was true, it was an admirable achievement on her part. She had discovered a way of keeping him afraid for years. Afraid in a way that, whether he chose to acknowledge it or not, had changed him. His increasingly antisocial behavior. Unexpected new feelings of anxious ambition, combined with conflict-avoidant behavior, which resulted in more Machiavellian tactics than he'd once thought himself capable of.

Miles still hadn't forgiven himself for "managing out" a promising young narrative designer who'd written to him privately with what struck Miles as overly political concerns about the platform's new privacy policies. To fix anything, Miles had argued, they needed time. Those policies earned them revenue, which bought them time. Without them, there'd be no opportunity for the ND's political concerns to be addressed, as there'd be no company. The complaints were ungrateful, if not pernicious, but they also weren't grounds on which he could fire the ND, and, in fact, Miles's role at the company required he be seen as encouraging of this level of candor. But more than alarming, the complaints were annoying, and they weren't going to go away anytime soon, so Miles had decided to approach the process of the ND's removal surgically, systematically dissolving responsibilities and therefore possibilities from the ND's daily life, like he was rerouting blood vessels from a vestigial organ, until the ND's career trajectory narrowed to a fine, static point, and he could no longer be viewed as an essential contributor to the future of the company, at which point the ND had chosen to quietly remove himself and pursue a more dynamic career elsewhere, and some small part of Miles's work life had resolved itself back to fine.

His plan for the ND had worked, but it wasn't a good

feeling. This wasn't Miles as he knew himself; it was a Miles whose time was running out. However much he disliked this new Miles, he couldn't help admiring his daughter for having done this to him, for having changed him so completely.

"I love you," he said.

"Ew," she said.

"I mean it," he said. "I love you very much."

"I know," she said. "So, like . . . easy."

"Sorry," he said. He sat a moment, considering the best way of broaching the subject of the threats. Maybe it was best just to come out with it. *You can just ask.* Maybe he should. He wished she would look up, if only a glance to let him know that she was still listening, that there was still a chance to get in a word and potentially turn this awkward time together into something more productive.

"She's not coming back," said his daughter. "Is she?"

"Who's that?" said Miles, genuinely confused.

"Mom," said his daughter, staring at the terrazzo. Staring, Miles realized, into the depths of where her mother now lived.

"No," he said, after a moment. "Or I don't know. The answer is, you don't need to worry about it."

"Well . . ." She turned the handle of her bag between her hands, sending several more drops to the floor. "I worry about it."

Miles felt the bristling tickle of the knot in his chest coming loose as she said it. Somehow, he'd done it. They were talking. It wasn't exactly what he wanted to be talking about, but she was telling him about something that upset her, and not just making sure he understood that she was upset. She was worried about her mom, and there were things he could say. If he was careful, he could fix this. But he had to choose his next move wisely.

Miles thought of the fortune-teller and the Côtes du Rhône. He thought of his daughter's mother, and realized that if he were to mention the death threats, if he were to put the question to her and force an answer after all this time, he would not only squander the opportunity of this moment, he also risked losing one of the few points of contact that remained between them. She had told him how she felt, and she was giving him a chance to respond in kind. She'd invited him to end their conversation with a volley toward future moments like these. Which, fewer and further between as they might be, was still more than nothing, though nothing more than this.

Miles knew what he needed to do. He realized then that he had been preparing for this for years. He had the tools. He knew the routine.

"Of course you worry," he said, doing his best to use a calming and neutral tone.

Finally, she looked up. She held his steady gaze.

"It's a completely valid and natural way to feel," he said. Miles rose gently and signaled to his daughter that she was welcome to hang her clothes if she wanted to. "And if you ever need to talk about it, I'm always here."

29

Miles stood alone in his office later that night, marveling at his creation. He had done well. For the first time in months, he felt accomplished. Now, and in the past. The Egg wasn't all him, but he had led them there. He'd pointed. His whole life he'd been faced with moments like this, moments that felt loaded with the potential to determine how the rest of his life would go. Taking a job. Having a child. Two children. Other Brians. The Egg. His daughter and their secret language. Each represented a branch leading him away from all the other possibilities, granting his triumphs the feeling of having been earned, and each wrong turn the nagging quality of having been avoidable.

It didn't bother Miles that he couldn't square his feeling that the future was unknowable to him with his sense that everything he'd ever done had led him to whatever moment he was in. Could a life's trajectory be both unpredictable and inevitable? He didn't know, and it didn't matter, because there would always be the undeniability of the thing he had created. He'd made choices, and they had changed things. They had brought him here.

The disassembling date had come and gone without a word from the company. Miles didn't believe they could have forgotten the Egg. It was too expensive, too secure, too integral to the company's new direction. If the Egg was still that, that is. The company's new direction.

If Miles had learned anything in the time he'd given them, it was that things could always change. Into what: it had once been Miles's job to answer that question. But now that it wasn't, he no longer had any real insight into what the fickle company's new response to an uneasy landscape might be. Things changed. They always had. It was up to the marketing team and PR coordinators to come up with a way of making it all sound like it made sense or was more than a series of well-funded if pendulous swings from one new direction to the next.

As far as the company was concerned, the Egg may very well have been obsolete. The future rarely looked the same for two days in a row. Miles didn't know, and he didn't mind not knowing. He honestly didn't. Miles understood and accepted—more than most of the successful people he'd met as the result of his success—that he didn't really know very much about life. He could accept this ego-disintegrating truth because he knew, on some level, that it didn't matter. In the end, all that really mattered was that he'd added to the landscape of human experience, forcing people to change in response to his alteration. What he'd done, and how he'd done it, was going to be the subject of discourse, intellectual interpretation, argument, and eventually government regulation.

Thanks to him, the world now knew what was possible, and that knowledge would one day be integrated, in one way or another, into all relevant industry discussions and forward-thinking strategies. At least for a while. He had influenced things, and influence trumped reality because influence was quantifiable, explainable, and human. And reality, at least as Miles figured it, extended so far beyond the human scale, he would never be able to truly see it for what it was, let alone comprehend whatever implications it had on his actual life. Miles could live with that. He didn't know very much in the end, but he knew bits and pieces. And bits and pieces were really all you needed to change things. People might argue with that, but he'd done it, so he could say it.

Miles's old fear was gathering itself outside the walls of his office, but in here there was only Miles, and the calm invitation of the Egg's unhinged jaw. Whether the company had de-prioritized its disassembling, or abandoned it altogether, it didn't matter. The future was a new idea, and there was always more money in a promise. But, whatever the company did next, whatever they did without him, they couldn't change the reality of the Egg. Whatever else happened, the Egg was here, staring back at Miles from the center of his office like the bisected head of a giant squid. It was objectively frightening, but he no longer felt afraid of it. He felt good. Life was not impossible, though it was hard. Talking with his daughter had left him feeling that headway was only a matter of time and focus. You had to meet your moment. You had to choose where to put your energy, and let it roll you as it would. You couldn't know what was coming. You could only choose where to put your energy. At one point in his life, he'd put his energy in the Egg. As a result, it was his. It was purely his own. By design, it was all he could think to want. He figured it was about time for him to want it.

Miles stepped into the mouth of the Egg and booted up *The Ghost Lover*.

the ghost lover

30

Miles walked the halls of his old home, astonished at the new program's clarity. The accuracy of it was making him feel sick. He'd heard of this—but it was rare. A small percentage of testers rejected the experience of the Egg on a physical level. Two parts of the brain went to war, feeling it was real versus knowing that it wasn't, with each insisting on the reality of what it perceived and neither being fully right. The failure of those two perceptive systems to resolve into a singular vision of reality triggered a third part of the brain to sound an alarm, forcing the body to evacuate, as it became convinced that the confusion was a result of illness or poison. Luckily for Miles, the company had gone to great pains to make the inside of the Egg waterproof, allowing for it to be hosed down after use.

Miles was worried he was headed that way until he started paying closer attention. The experience was brilliantly detailed, lending depth and clarity to a memory he'd been all but set to lose, but the more he looked, the more he began to see that the details were too specific, too perfect, to be real. They appeared real at first glance, but

Miles was already starting to identify the small ways in which they were out of sync with reality as he experienced it. For example, the photos on the shelves looked right—they *felt* right—but he knew they couldn't be the ones he and his wife had chosen when they were decorating the house. These photos were all too poignant. There was his daughter's birth photo. Miles and his wife in a pile in the woods. These were memories of photos he'd seen, but they couldn't have been the ones that had actually lined their shelves. The selections didn't have that arbitrary quality, the lack of immediate resonance Miles had come to associate with walking the halls of his old home, at least as he remembered it. The shade of pale blue in their bedroom was closer to the way the color had felt to him the day they'd selected it, the day they'd fallen in love with it, which was suspicious to him, because nothing in life was really like that: as good as you remembered it. The rendering was closer to what Miles wanted than what was true. And as soon as Miles realized that, ironically, he felt better.

This level of accuracy was never his intention with *The Ghost Lover*. The experience was designed to suggest, not convince. Miles knew it didn't matter what he'd meant to do, especially at this point, but he was happy to carry his objections deeper into the experience, putting distance between him and its more convincing aspects, and indirectly soothing his stomach.

Soon, Miles stood at the foot of his old bed, listening to the thumps in the wall. His ghost. He didn't have an ex who came readily to mind, but whoever it was, they were noisy and shifting, just like they had been all those years before.

Miles was about to climb over the bed and settle up to the thumps, but a door opened deep within the house. He heard his daughters talking in their room. Not shrieking. Not fighting. Not even whispering conspiratorially. Their voices were steady and undisturbed by his presence, as if their personalities had been scrubbed. Or they were somehow, miraculously, momentarily, getting along. He hurried to meet them.

Miles caught his ten-year-old entering the kitchen, headed for the fridge door. She lifted the top half of the paper he'd magneted there years before, nearly exposing the first threat, technically the second.

"No, no, no," he said, guiding away her hand, but not before catching a glimpse of the handwriting on the lower half of the note. It was handwriting he recognized, though not from the threats. This was the handwriting he'd seen on checks and notes, failed attempts at journaling. It was the nearly indecipherable scrawl that had followed him all his life, obscuring messages to parents, engendering laughter and doubt from his coworkers during white board presentations.

TALK TO LILY AT WORK. MAKE HER
FEEL APPRECIATED.

DO SOMETHING NICE FOR CLAIRE.
DO SOMETHING SHE'D LIKE.

READ MORE. FINISH WHAT YOU
START.

FIND A MEDICAL APPLICATION FOR
THE EGG.

They were notes to himself, in his own handwriting. Notes he'd never written, but, apparently, had.

"I'm sorry," said his ten-year-old. "I like the paper."

There was nothing sinister in her voice. Nothing cruel or strange. She was smiling without a secret.

"It's okay," he said. "It's all right."

He knelt before her, and she stared back at him, waiting patiently for whatever it was he had to say.

"I would never hurt you," he said. "What happened in the Egg, that wasn't real. It was a game gone wrong. If you ever have the chance to see it, don't look."

"I know," she said. "I won't. Thank you." She said it plainly, matter-of-factly, as if he'd been reminding her of something so banal as to turn off the lights when she was leaving her room, or to collect the water glasses on her floor and take them to the sink.

"Okay," he said. "Good. All right."

For a moment, Miles was mist. The relief of their brief conversation was total, and in the face of that totality, he felt weak and unable to move.

"And you were sending me the notes," he said. "The threats. Leaving them in the hallway, right?"

"Right," she said. "I was sending you the notes. It was our own secret language."

"You scared me, you know," he said. "A little. But you did."

"I didn't mean to scare you," she said. "I thought you'd laugh."

"It was funny!" he said, wiping his eye with his wrist. "And a little scary."

His ten-year-old smiled. Not eerily. Not falsely. She smiled like a child in a picture. Like a child who was only trying to tell him one thing; that this is how she looked when she was happy. She looked at him like that for several seconds, then vanished into the nearby wall.

Miles headed back to the bedroom and climbed over his old mattress, placing his ear just above the headboard. That was where the thumps were always loudest. His knees pressed into the clumpy pillow he'd refused to replace out of principle—what use were new pillows, he'd argued, when all he wanted was consistency?

He moved his cheek along the wall, until he could feel the thumps of the ghost in his jaw. He could smell the lamb too, just as he remembered it. He checked his nail and found the rice.

"Hello?" he said, into the wall.

The thumps stopped.

"Hello," said a voice he knew. A voice he'd known for more than half his life.

"Claire?" he said.

"Miles," she said.

"You're not an ex," he said, remembering only then that she was.

"I'm the ghost," she said.

"It's not right," he said.

"I left," she said.

"You said you didn't," he said. "You're in the basement."

"No," she said. "I'm in the wall."

Then the bed was gone. Miles was bathed in light from an orange spot, leaning against a bar made from plywood set over six spent kegs. It was a detail from a house party—the only one he could remember having gone to with Claire.

She was standing beside him, too nervous to lean on the makeshift bar. She wasn't his wife. She was a woman who worked in wardrobe. A woman who liked the cold. His wife hated the cold, but Claire had loved it. She took jacketless walks in the snow. She watched the flakes melt into her hair in the bathroom mirror, the cool water beading down her cheeks.

"I told you I was going to hurt you," she said.

"You said you were going to be mean to me," he said. "That's different."

"I was in my twenties," she said. "The message got scrambled."

Claire was silent then, so Miles made her cry. This was a big moment, he thought, and he'd never seen her cry before. He couldn't remember when he'd stopped admiring that about her.

"Tell me about your childhood," he said. "Tell me what happened."

"If I told you it was bad," she said, "would you believe me?"

"It was bad?" he said.

"Put it this way," she said, "you should believe me."

Miles realized he didn't know the details of her childhood, so he couldn't convincingly work them into the rendering. He resisted the urge to populate his ghost lover with his own weak assumptions. Domestic violence, sexual abuse, bulimia, cutting, isolation, bullying—clichés for a reason, and things he knew he was only thinking of because he'd seen them on television. He'd researched them for television writers. But whatever he was picturing, he knew it wasn't the truth of what had happened to his wife, or at least how she'd experienced it. He knew because that wasn't the way his life worked—he was never right when it came to understanding what she was going through.

"Am I a goat?" he asked.

She smiled. The narrow beds between her teeth were stained red.

"Am I?" he said.

"You're good," she said.

Miles turned to hide a wince and found himself spinning a loop in his office chair. The place was empty, populated only with chairs and chairs and chairs and tables. He fiddled with the jaw of the Godzilla head on his desk, thinking about something nice he'd done for his wife. It was something she'd liked. He wasn't sure what it was—he'd done it earlier and couldn't remember now—but he could feel the warmth of her appreciation radiating through him. He'd done something right, he knew that. It was going to be a good day.

"I'm back," said Lily, appearing in blue and white lines at the edge of his desk. She should have approached him from behind, or walked out of the bathroom, drying her hands on her jeans. But of course it would be Lily that glitched in some way. It was so typically her to expose the artificiality in whatever it was that he was feeling. To fill him with self-doubt and make him question what was in front of him, even in the Egg.

"Like you never left," said Miles.

"Here I am," said Lily. She raised her hands, palms to the air. "Never fucking left."

"You think I'm an asshole," he said.

"You are an asshole," she said.

"What's your son's name?" he said.

"I was fucking with you," she said.

"Oh," he said.

"Or am I now?" she said.

He stared at her. He studied her strange chin.

"You know I'm sorry," he said.

"Yeah," she said.

"Do you really know that?" he said.

"Fuck yeah, I do!" she said, bobbing her bangs so they bounced.

"I always liked her." His wife was hidden among the

costume racks behind him, hanging jackets. He could see her through the rattling metal, the lines of fabric slicing her up like floor-to-ceiling blinds. "Lily, I mean."

"You never met her," he said.

"But she's good for you," she said. "She keeps you on your toes."

"Maybe," said Miles. "But she's gone. And you're gone."

"I'm right here," said his wife. She headed to the far end of the rack to zip the dust bag into place. "You can't miss me."

"They fired me," he said.

"So, enjoy yourself," she said.

"How?" he said.

"Figure it out," she said.

"For something I didn't do," he said. "Something it looked like I did, depending on who was looking. It's almost funny."

His wife, soon to be his ex-wife, but his wife here, in the Egg, smiled. She touched him. There was nothing but warmth in her implausible words.

"Even if you did," she said. "It's okay."

"Even if I did?" he said. "What's that supposed to mean?"

"It's a human-enough flaw to be forgiven this once," she said. "If you did."

"But I didn't," he said.

She smiled. She touched him.

"It's not true," he said.

"It's not true," she said.

"I didn't," he said,

"You didn't," she said.

"You're a sex pervert," he said.

The racks were wiped, and his wife was gone. He stood before the scandalized civil rights lawyer, a man he'd never seen before in person but still made several inches taller than himself. The man stoically received Miles's accusation before a crowd of faceless millions. Miles heard them in the distance, shuffling their feet.

"I'm a sex pervert," said the scandalized civil rights lawyer.

"And a creep," said Miles.

"Yes," said the scandalized civil rights lawyer. "It's worse than you've heard. I've done unforgivable things."

Miles was running out of steam. Dramatic as it all was, these were still impoverished dreams. Even this confrontation, however unlikely, was something he could probably have accomplished in real life. A conversation he might have had, if he gave the project enough time and effort.

Miles searched the scandalized civil rights lawyer for a sign of how to proceed, and he saw only blank admission. Where were the others? Someone should have changed this by now. A wooden bench creaked in the distance. Millions of heels whispered dust along the floor. Miles didn't want the man to be guilty, but he did want clarity. He could make him confess a thousand times, and he still wouldn't have that. Looking at the scandalized civil rights lawyer now, the unknown depths of the man's depravity stared back at Miles like a lake.

Miles set his hand on the neck of the blank man before him. He squeezed, awkwardly choking the scandalized civil rights lawyer until he could get his grip right. They were standing, and then the man was on his back and Miles was over him. The man's throat was a knot of smooth rope, and Miles squeezed it, trying to undo the knot with the ends of his fingers, working at it until the eyes of his victim popped red, filling with blood.

The deed done, the body still, Miles stood, wondering if this was how a choked person would actually look. He couldn't know, as he'd never choked anyone. He'd imagined it would be gruesome, but gore turned his stomach. Red-eyed, the scandalized civil rights lawyer looked more comical than dead. Like an actor trying not to breathe. After a moment, Miles let him stand up and brush off the assault. The blood seeped back from his sockets, escaping into his skull as if through several small drains, until the eyes of the scandalized civil rights lawyer were blue and white again, as they'd been in the pictures on the junk mail Miles received almost daily.

The scandalized civil rights lawyer blinked his way out of the room, and millions filed out behind him, neither disappointed nor impressed. Looking closely, Miles saw that they were nurses. Rows and rows of nurses guiding men and women in medical gowns into an endless line of Eggs. His machines. The men and women were smiling, eager to experience the medical application he'd discovered for it.

"Thank you," they said, one after the other.

Miles reached out, lifting a fire poker from the ribs of his six-year-old.

"Thank you," she said, brushing cabin dust from her sunburned arms.

Miles wiped it all away, and his old house took new shape around him. He heard the thumps again, but this time he ignored them. He headed for the office. Answers, desires, hope, nostalgia, pleasure, satisfaction—it was starting to depress him. Here was everything he could think to ask for, and all it had done was remind him of the unsolved problems waiting for him just beyond the edges of the machine.

The pleasures it provided had only served to underline Miles's creeping suspicion that his life was becoming unmanageable. A single present sentence from his daughter had been enough to make him feel invincible. It felt suddenly so pathetic. His life felt small, and far from him, and the comforts of the machine were being converted directly into back fat.

Miles was spiraling without a hotline. He needed the feeling to lift, if only for a second. The machine was making things worse. He felt worse. And he felt jealous. Not because the Egg didn't work, but because it might have worked. Because it didn't work for him.

Now that he had seen it all, there was only really one thing he wanted. He'd glimpsed its idea in the Egg, but he had not found it there. Miles did not want the quick, clear resolution of each individual problem in his life. He could manage them on his own, with enough time, enough money. What Miles wanted was for the inevitability of the next big problem in his life to be removed. To not exist. Not just his awareness of it—but its reality. He wanted to feel, to know, and to be confident in knowing, if only for a moment, that things weren't simply and unavoidably going to get worse.

Miles crossed through the red dirt outside a rural cabin in Texas, kicking old ants with new boots. He stood before the Egg in the projection of his home. Disappointing as it was, the machine had still given him the impression of hope. Hope that he might hope again. That's what disappointment was, after all. The hope that something else was possible. It wasn't the Egg's fault that he couldn't sustain those feelings, that he couldn't shake his lingering awareness of the problems of his life. They were too close to the skin, too much a part of him. To be rid of them, he needed to shed them and start again. It was a problem of perspective. He knew too much, or not enough. He couldn't be sure. He only knew that things were off.

When his projection of the Egg opened, its interior was stupidly cheetah print. Miles laughed in the impression of his office. He liked the things he came up with when he was on his own, even if they didn't satisfy him. Or not yet. There was hope that they would. There was hope because he was starting to understand what exactly it was that he wanted, and how to ask for it. If he went deeper, perhaps he could draw himself further from the nagging awareness that was eating at his joy. He could wrap himself in possibility, quiet the humming layers of his mind. It was there, somewhere. He could reach for it.

Miles climbed into the Egg within the Egg, wanting nothing. Miles wanted nothing, and to be absolved, if only briefly, of his capacity to screw it up.

31

Miles had to admit he felt better. Not all the way better, but better than he'd felt, really, since the arrival of the first note—technically the second. It hadn't felt like a turning point at the time—and it certainly hadn't turned him in the direction the notes seemed to portend—but, thinking back on it, that evening in the kitchen with the first/second note occurred to him as one that marked the beginning of a new phase in his life, which only now, in this silent, empty place, was starting to feel in any way resolved.

The experience was empty. A chamber so perfect, so precise, its edges were undetectable. And Miles felt better. He felt proud. Proud to have changed the world and, after all this time, to find at the heart of his own creation the only thing he had ever truly been after. Not a Band-Aid. Not a promise. Relief.

He tried to move, but there was no body in the chamber. He tried to speak, but again, there was nothing with which to speak. It was an odd sensation, and he struggled to describe it, even to himself.

If death was like this, Miles thought. Maybe. Maybe, he could stand it. Or even look forward to it. Then again, if the relief he was experiencing was contingent on the guarantee that he was in fact not dead—that he had the option to return to his actual life, with what was left of his family, at any moment—it seemed to follow that the absence of that guarantee would turn tranquil isolation into a nightmare. If he brought with him the memories of what he'd left behind but had no recourse to return to them—only memories to consult on the far side of a shuttered Egg—it was hard to think of anything more depressing. He amended his thought. If death was like this, but without memory, *then* maybe he could stand it. Maybe. But the memories he had did seem to be a critical part of the relief he was feeling. From what was he relieved, if not from those memories he'd brought into the experience with him? If his memory of the memories he'd brought into the Egg was gone, the experience—his experience—would be of nothing, but with no awareness of it as such, as there would no longer be anything with which to compare it. Nothing, and nothing from which to be relieved. A loading screen. All potential. And if, having memories, he was relieved to be away from the life that had formed them, not having memories could work the other way—he'd want out. It was worse than depressing—it was terrifying. The thought of death not as the easy absence of life, but as a living prison.

Miles realized a machine that manifested his desires as they occurred to him wasn't the safest place in which to contemplate his preparedness for death—especially a death so close to his own personal vision of hell. But the machine was designed to closely monitor its impact on the living engine. It wouldn't let him die. And if hell came about, he could change it back. Or, eventually, someone else would.

Getting users to accept that reality of the platform was going to be an essential part of successfully integrating the Egg, at least if the early chaos of the shared experiences had any hope of achieving the uneasy balance Miles had once predicted. Uneasy because it would necessitate a willingness on behalf of users to cede control of their experience to a host of infinite strangers, which anyone could see would be a tough pill to swallow, though only for people of a certain age. Aside from scattered detractors, Miles had been confident users would eventually thrive on the platform, happy to meet others somewhere in the middle. It would be easier for those who'd grown up with it. Those who had no sense of what the world had been like before the Egg. That eventuality had been borne out in CI testing, where they'd been able to watch in real time the number of users ideologically opposed to the concept of the shared experience dwindling, as new, younger users poured in. It had made Miles excited for the future, excited to see it come to be, though his own daughters had never used the headsets and were terrified of the Egg.

It didn't matter. Maya was swimming, and Mia had become obsessed with birds. She seemed to know everything there was to know about each of the species they could see from their property, and she'd learned to summon more to the house with different seeds and elixirs. Miles was blown away by her recall. He'd been confronted with it for more than a decade now, but it was no less incredible to him that her experiences were being recorded somewhere, stored for later use, and that she was mastering her ability to call upon them. Personhood, from out of nowhere, slowly taking shape before his eyes. He knew he should enjoy it while he could, before she learned to lock it all away inside a baffling human. The second she crystallized, he would lose her. It had already happened with Maya. She was gone, and Mia was going. He could see it in her eyes every time a bird took flight. She looked happy for them. Like they were doing something sublime, just leaving.

Miles had never cared about birds, but he wanted to know what his daughter knew. When he asked the right questions, she would sometimes tell him about the ones she'd drawn to their backyard. How they danced and why. Not just to draw one another in, but to open themselves up to another's approach. A protocol for actively sharing what had once been private. Personal. It was a performance of vulnerability, inviting in a stranger with a display of tender zones.

"Why birds?" he'd asked her on a day when he was running out of questions, but she was being particularly generous with her time.

"Because birds," she'd explained, without looking away from her binoculars, "eat ants."

✦

Miles missed his children. He missed his children, and he missed talking to his wife about them. He missed Claire. He owed her an apology, and he owed her acceptance. Even if he was still angry. Even if he would forever remain confused, he still could have done the reading. As a gesture. Maybe it wouldn't have changed things, but at least he would feel better about himself. He could take away the ammunition and maybe that would get them closer to something. Help him see her more clearly, at least. It was easier to understand that in the Egg, where reality was just out of reach. It was almost funny. He hadn't found anything in the Egg but a moment's peace, and in that peace he had hurriedly returned to the life he'd left behind. He would have laughed, if he'd been there to do so. After all the years he'd spent dreading the actualization of a series of toothless death threats, here he was—willingly giving up small pieces of what was left of his time on earth to an empty machine, just so he could experience what it felt like to be free of them. It was absurd. But it had worked. Nothingness, self-imposed. Miles did feel better. It had been a useful experiment. But now that it was over, Miles wanted something again.

Miles wanted out.

✦

Miles tried to have the thought more clearly. That he was ready to leave. Ready to get back to what was left of his life. That that's what he wanted to happen. As clear as his thoughts were, none of them amounted to anything. Miles wanted and tried. And nothing changed.

32

Ending an experience was supposed to be easy. The machines were designed to be hyperresponsive, tailored to the individual user. Over time, and with repeated use, the machines could even map, then anticipate, common impulses, engendering a response more or less the moment you had the thought, with increasingly predictive speed. That was the plan anyway. But Miles had been ready to go since he'd thought of his daughter and the birds. He'd wanted out—he still wanted out—but he was nowhere. With no one. It didn't worry him, but it was weird.

Miles tried to sit up. He thought of reaching for the edges of the machine. He pictured his arms, wrenching left and right. Wriggling. Reaching and kicking. The feeling of white snow held. He opened his mouth, or what he pictured as his mouth, and nothing happened. It was the idea of a mouth. The thought of something he could use. He thought of his wife. He thought of Claire, and the man who'd convinced her she could live without the sun. He thought of Claire and the girls, and nothing happened.

Miles stopped reaching. He focused on remembering

the edges of the machine. He knew they were there. He pictured himself pulling at them. He pictured his bewildering home. Walls that didn't add up. Hallways that curved back to where they started. At the heart of it all was the Egg. A crew was coming to disassemble it. A team was coming to pull the wires from the walls. He pictured himself pulling his body out of the machine and into his office. Into his living room, where pillars of granite stood wrapped in vines crawling through acrylic slats in the floor. His home was gone, but it was also there, he was certain of it, beyond the edges of this immeasurable space. His house as it was, not as it had been. The harder he tried to get out, the easier it seemed to be for the experience to hold him. The distance between what he knew and where he was felt infinite. But Miles had built this place, so he knew it had limits. He'd seen them.

✦

Miles wasn't dead. This was the closest he'd ever come to it, but he would get out of this and back to his life. He would hand over the notes in his closet. Liquidate his stock. He would buy the cow from the farm up north and milk it every other day. However often you were supposed to milk a cow. He'd call it by its first, real name. A name that was on a chalkboard somewhere. Miles couldn't remember it, but he knew he'd read it. He'd read the name out loud, and the cow had looked at him. Miles reached for the edges of the machine. He reached for nothing with nothing. He knew the absence of his hands in a memory. They'd been his, and he had used them.

✦

Miles knew this wasn't it, because what a waste. He was only getting started. There was plenty left to do. Plenty he hadn't thought of.

But if this *was* it—if this was really the end—then there was more to it than he'd ever imagined there would be. He still had time to think. Time to find a good thought on which to rest. Time for the idea of his daughter in the water. The other in the air. Claire, his wife, and the edges of the machine. The harder he searched, the less they seemed to exist. His teenager. His ten-year-old. His six-year-old. Like a hermit crab, Mia slid into the designations Maya left behind. He told himself not to think of their names. He remembered what could happen. What could go wrong. He tried to put them out of his mind.

This wasn't it, because here he was. He was nowhere, but still Miles. Still afraid. That's how he knew. Miles's fear held him to himself, and he remembered now—this was a horrible place. This was only a reminder. In the absence of what had been, he was alone with its loss. The machine had no edges, but it was still a machine. A world he'd built that had built this for him. The illusion of a grave of his own design. Temporary, in any case.

Because this wasn't what he wanted.

Although, he remembered, it had been. It kind of had been. He'd had the thought, at least. Nothing, with no ability to make it worse. No ability to make it something. Maybe this was the desire the machine had detected beneath Miles's pathetic attempts to gather the unraveling threads of his life, picking at them as they unwound, pinching them together, insisting these broken things were what could give his life meaning, what he was terrified of losing. And if this was what was underneath all his grotesque and unprofitable efforts, maybe there was something to it. Something to nothing. Or something to be gained from experiencing it at least. Maybe the machine had done its job exactly as they'd designed it. Here was the world Miles had wanted for himself. Here was all he could ever think to want.

It was an appealing idea, that this was all born of his intention. That hell was more than heaven; it was a heaven of his own design. At the same time, it was hard to fully abandon the thought of someone standing over him, watching him wriggle and fight. That was part of the design too, after all—other people. What was happening to him now could be the next big thing. Soon to be a massive hit. Miles, struggling for the edges of the machine. Miles, thinking of moving. Convincing himself that this was what he'd wanted all along. Miles, giving in.

Maya was going. Mia would soon be too. Claire had eased into a bunker with the stranger who'd built it. He shouldn't be thinking of them here, but he wanted to remember. To be gone, they had to have been there. This was a reminder. Miles was something—not nothing—and the choice was still his. Miles opened the idea of his eye, and the options appeared before him, like pillars of hope on a translucent screen.

BEG

DANCE

OR DIE

ACKNOWLEDGMENTS

While working on this book, I had the encouragement and support of many people, without whom *Users* would not exist as it does. To start, I'd like to thank Mensah Demary, Wah-Ming Chang, Cecilia Flores, Lena Moses-Schmitt, Megan Fishmann, Gregg Kulick, Lexi Earle, and everyone else at Soft Skull/Catapult, for all they've done to make this book a reality.

Thank you to Daniel Levin Becker (who has read these pages many, many times, and is no doubt so sick of reading them that he might never come across this inscription), as well as to Casey Jarman, Kyle Morton, Daniel Pearce, Chris Taylor, Michael Dawson, Jordan Bass, Sam Cook, Jen Gann, and Walker Smart. To my writing group—Ingrid Rojas Contreras, Anisse Gross, Rachel Khong, R. O. Kwon, Caille Milner, Margaret Wilkerson Sexton, and Esmé Weijun Wang—thank you for years of honesty, comradery, and song. Thank you to Clara Sankey (who is owed an overdue double-thanks), and to my mother, Julie Winnette (for her love, her support, and her stories).

ACKNOWLEDGMENTS

I'd like to thank Cille Lansade and the good people at Le Château de Monthelon, where I spent several weeks developing the ideas that would result in this book's early pages.

I also owe a debt to Amelia Gray, whose novel *Threats* taught me many things, including the raw power of a few, intimidating words.

And thank you to my early supporters, all novelists I greatly admire, and whose kind words mean more than I have room to express on an acknowledgments page: Hernan Diaz, Esmé Weijun Wang, Jeff Vandermeer, and Andrew Sean Greer.

Thank you to Sarah Cassavant and Alyson Sinclair, and to my agent Kevin O'Connor, for his unwavering support.

And, finally, thank you to Andi Winnette: my greatest critic, my most trusted confidant, my home. I love you, bug.

COLIN WINNETTE is the author of several books, including the award-winning indie bestseller *Coyote* and *Haints Stay*. His most recent novel, *The Job of the Wasp*, was published by Soft Skull Press in 2018 and was an American Booksellers Association Indie Next Pick. Winnette was the winner of Les Figues Press's NOS Book Contest, a runner-up for Cleveland State University Poetry Center's First Book Award, and a finalist for *Gulf Coast Magazine*'s Donald Barthelme Prize for Short Prose. His writing has appeared in numerous publications, including *Playboy*, *McSweeney's*, *The Believer*, *The Paris Review Daily*, and more. A former bookseller in Texas, Vermont, New York, and California, he is now a writer living in San Francisco.